THE DEMANDS OF THE FLESH

Also by March Hastings

THE DEMANDS OF THE FLESH

MARCH HASTINGS

CUTTING EDGE

ISBN-13: 978-1-952138-82-9

Published by
Cutting Edge Books
PO Box 8212
Calabasas, CA 91372
www.cuttingedgebooks.com

CHAPTER ONE

S HE heard quick steps moving up behind her in the corridor. The touch of a young man's palm on Ellen's forearm made her breath catch. She looked up into brown eyes that smiled reassuringly.

"You're Mrs. Tendler, aren't you?" His voice was warm as his eyes. "Warren Junior's mother?"

"Yes," she answered uncertainly. If he would only take his hand away. Not since Warren's death had a man touched her. Three years. And now her nerves leaped with a sudden jolting that made her ashamed.

"I'm Jay Masters. Warren's in my class this term." He kept his long stride in step with her own. "I've been looking forward to meeting you."

"If you're going to tell me that Warren has a record of being late…"

"No, no," he laughed. "Nothing of the sort."

They came out onto the steps of the school and stood looking at each other in the sunlight. A touch of gold teased his hair with vivacity.

"I just wanted to have a chat with you before the semester begins. A mother's point of view can be very helpful." His voice did not accuse her for neglecting to attend Open School Week or Parent-Teacher meetings.

"Yes," she said. "I'd love to have a talk with you."

She waited for him to make the next suggestion. They could go to the coffee shop across the street. Or did he know that she would prefer a cafe? Alcohol could not quench the desperate thirst in her body. But a few cocktails with dinner or a highball before going to bed was all the company she could permit herself. And sometimes, drink eased the memory of Warren's kisses.

"If you have time," Ellen said hesitantly, "we can go to my place. It's not very far."

"Fine," he said. "I'd like that."

They strolled beneath the canopy of maples toward Ellen's car. Autumn tones of russet and orange painted an Indian summer around them. She heard the sound of her shoes on the crisp leaves and inhaled the heavy laden fragrance. Just as those leaves died only to be reborn, so Ellen's heart responded with its need to bloom once again. Ellen felt glad that she had ventured out today.

She drove the long convertible with an accustomed grace. Her slim fingers in their long black kid gloves barely touched the wheel and she felt Jay Masters watching them.

"Wonderful thing, power steering," she said lightly. She didn't want to ride with him sitting quietly beside her. There must be conversation to keep her thoughts from galloping into forbidden places.

"I drive a '49 Chevvy myself," Mr. Masters said. "It's kind of like an old grandpaw. Willing, but not very able."

Ellen felt herself beginning to relax. He didn't seem like a school teacher at all. No severity or prudishness tainted him. Perhaps with Jay Masters' help, Warrie would begin to straighten out a little bit.

They reached the outskirts of town and Ellen stopped the car in front of the stone ranch house. Other private homes lined the dead end street; but none of them had such well-trimmed lawns or spacious design. Ellen kept her home an immaculate tribute to her dead husband.

"You have a lovely place," Jay Masters said when she had closed the door behind him.

For a moment they stood in silence. Warrie was out playing ball. The maid came in every other day and this was an off afternoon. Alone with this tall young man dressed in easy tweeds, Ellen felt not at all like a matron. Something about his smile made her conscious of her own vitality. And, though Ellen hid her body beneath conservative suits, it throbbed with a desire to be seen, touched, loved.

"We'll be comfortable on the back terrace," she said. "I'll get us a pot of tea." She wanted to be alone for a minute to smooth the wind blown hair and retouch her lipstick. Perhaps Jay Masters was a happily married man who couldn't care less about her appearance. But this didn't seem likely.

He allowed her to settle him in a wicker chair that overlooked sprawling hills toward the blue-green horizon. Ellen watched him cross his ankles on a hassock and take out his briarwood pipe.

"This is the life," he grinned, The squared cheek bones and thick shoulders added a live touch of masculinity to the empty house.

"I'll be back in a moment," Ellen said.

She hurried off to the kitchen and set a kettle onto the electric range. Then she opened the refrigerator door and stared at the bits and scraps. She had neglected to go shopping. For the first time, it occurred to Ellen that the refrigerator never really did have much in it. Since Warren's accident, she hadn't cared to eat at home. The desire to bake pies or roast beef on Sundays was buried with her husband. This lovely, rambling house that he had left her was like a hollow heart.

But she must find something to serve Jay Masters. Spurred on by her embarrassment, Ellen foraged in all the cupboards and managed to fix a tray of deviled ham and cheese sandwiches. As she folded napkins and set the tea cups, a warm glow began to suffuse her. For some strange reason, she was feeling at home in her own kitchen. Excitement mingled with an undercurrent of contentment. The spell of three years of mourning began to thaw.

Quickly she went to the washroom and put a few touches of powder on her nose and forehead. She tilted her chin upward and dabbed cologne along her throat. A pang of guilt slowed her hand as she remembered that Jay Masters had not come here to admire her. But nevertheless she combed the whisps of bangs more evenly on her forehead and brushed up her eyebrows, impelled by the strength of her loneliness.

The sound of bubbling water brought her back to the kitchen and she returned to Jay Masters happily laden with her tray of offerings.

The sweet aroma of tobacco mingled comfortably with the snack. Jay Masters put his pipe aside and gladly accepted half of a sandwich. She watched him eat with a healthy and boyish appetite that complimented her more than any words of praise.

Only after he had finished did he recall the purpose of his visit. With the cup sitting half empty on his lap, he said, "I hope you don't mind if I speak frankly about your boy."

"Not at all." She felt instinctively that he would not embarrass her. "You know I want to do everything possible to help Warren adjust. He's not a rebellious child by nature."

"Of course he isn't. I've watched him in the school yard. When the other boys talk about going fishing with their dads, Warren becomes full of bravado. That's how he makes up for it, I guess." He waited as Ellen opened a cigarette box, then struck a match and held its flame toward her. "If he were a girl, your job would be a lot easier."

"Perhaps I haven't really tried hard enough," she answered honestly.

"Well, here's what I have in mind," he said with a practical tone that lent Ellen new spirit. "I'm going to organize a camping group and make Warren second in charge. During the week, I'd like you to work with him on last term's arithmetic and grammar.

I'll make up an outline of the lessons for you. Perhaps between us, he can get back into the swing."

"I don't know how to thank you," Ellen said softly.

"Don't do that," he grinned. "I need something to keep myself occupied on weekends too. This is a very small town, Mrs. Tendler. A person has to build his own fire or die out."

She took the cup from him, watching the heavy college ring glint on his finger. He had the ruggedness of a woodsman in those hands. No doubt sleeping under the stars would be a second home to him. A boy could learn much of manly goodness from this person. and a woman, what could he teach a woman? If those broad fingers dug into the flesh of her body, what passion could she discover? The gentleness of his lips might discover the secrets of her desire and fulfill them.

Ellen thrust these thoughts brutally from her and refilled his cup with the steaming liquid.

"No thank you," he said. "I've got a lot of work to do yet this evening. Please don't tempt me to stay on."

"All right. I've got to pick up Warren anyway. We'll ride back to town together." She left the tea things and gathered her gloves and keys.

Ellen drove quickly now, enjoying the coolness of the wind against her neck. They chatted about Warren and Ellen revealed little things about her married life which might help Jay to understand the boy. He listened with interest as Ellen spoke about the wood working shop set up in the basement. Even the maid did not go down there to dust.

"It's a pity to let all that go to waste," Jay said.

"But Warren's too young for saws," she protested.

He did not argue the point, but Ellen felt that he did not agree with her either. She wondered what it would be like to have an honest to goodness fight with the man. To watch those fine eyes flashing heatedly and see that gentle mouth drawn into a stubborn line that would not yield. How delicious.

All too soon they reached the wooden house in which Jay Masters rented three rooms. He stood for one second with his hand resting on the door of the car.

"Tomorrow then?" he said. "What time will be convenient for you?"

"Seven o'clock."

"I'll be there."

He waved as she swung the car around the corner.

Ellen drove slowly around the town thinking that perhaps she should try to find Warrie. She never did call for him because he resented any little action that might make him feel like a momma's boy. Warrie came and went as he pleased and until today Ellen had been trusting to God that her son would find some kind of discipline more effective than herself. Jay Masters seemed to her like a present from heaven. She felt that his interest in the boy was sincere. He loved children and he responded with sympathy to Warrie's trouble. For this alone, Jay Masters was a true friend. She would do everything possible to be worthy.

The experience stirred Ellen with a vague restlessness. She did not want to return to the silent house and ponder her thoughts. She needed some kind of outlet for her dormant energies. To sit and to drink and to consider could hardly be satisfying now. Her body, her nerves required action like a colt too long penned in the stable.

She parked the car and decided to shop for some groceries. Tomorrow she would not be embarrassed again. The main street was filled with strolling neighbors carrying their own bundles or scolding babies for spilling ice cream. Unlike most, Ellen knew very little about the private lives of the people to whom she nodded hello. Ellen's mind did not have a flair for prying. Nor did she wish to become too friendly with most of the women. Ellen had hardly anything in common with the happy homemakers. Because her reputation was important for Warrie's sake, she could not join the activities of the wild ones who were as lost as herself. Planted as though on an island, Ellen had preferred to remain by herself until things somehow worked out. Now Jay Masters had come to build her bridge back toward the community. She lifted her face to the sun and felt it warm her closed eyelids.

"Well, look who's out in the daytime."

Ellen turned to the devilish lilting voice that made her grin in response. A chubby, freckled woman who could be forty but would never look a day over seventeen offered Ellen a piece of gum. Still smiling, Ellen shook her head no to the gum.

"Come on, kid, live it up a little." She unwrapped the gum and made Ellen take it.

"How've you been, Sandy?"

"Desperate, of course. Come on, I'll buy you a drink so you can cry into it for me."

Ellen had a special affection for this woman because she had met Warren at one of Sandy's parties. Her enormous joy made every day seem like a new golden opportunity. Ellen did not wish to avoid her now. Sandy's energetic humor was just what she needed.

"Okay," Ellen said. "But let me get some supper things first."

"Pish tash, supper." Her taffy colored hair bounced in reckless curls. "You'll come have supper with us."

Ellen allowed herself to be led into the small clean bar which was her favorite. She didn't really feel like shopping anyhow. Warrie always ate supper in the luncheonette where he could get bacon and tomato sandwiches the way he liked them.

They found a booth toward the rear and Sandy ordered V. O. and water for them both.

"So why are you looking this marvelous, Ellen girl? Go on, look at yourself. You're putting me to shame."

Despite herself, Ellen felt the beginnings of a blush in her cheeks.

"All right," Sandy laughed. "Don't tell me. I can wait till you're drunk."

"Oh no," Ellen said. "One and that's it."

"Two?"

"One." She opened her purse and glanced at the pocket watch that had been Warren's. "I'm starting a new schedule." She felt pleased with herself and the satisfaction glowed in her voice. Of course her resolution was premature. She couldn't count on Jay Masters becoming her friend. But she had been looking for an excuse to start living again. And he had for the moment given her that.

"Well," Sandy said. "Whatever it is that's happening, I'm glad for you."

Ellen took Sandy's hand and squeezed it impulsively. She didn't want to shut Sandy out. But how foolish it would be to tell her about this afternoon when nothing had actually happened. Perhaps it was foolish to place so much importance on Jay Masters' interest in Warrie. She felt strangely unprotected and like a school child herself. The years of fighting off her natural feminine desires made her terribly vulnerable. And her loneliness magnified even the most innocent of approaches. Good sense told her to forget Jay Masters except in his role of teacher.

"Look," Ellen said. "Why don't we have dinner together this Friday? And bring Henry too."

"I'd love that," Sandy said, examining her empty glass. "But my brother Raoul is coming in from New York tonight. We're having a little party for him Friday. Why don't you come over to us?"

Why not indeed, Ellen thought. She hadn't seen Raoul since her marriage. He had been a good loser when Ellen had turned down his proposal. Instead of making a spectacle of his disappointment, he'd gone to New York, finished law school and set up practice. From little things that Sandy mentioned, he was quite successful and still a bachelor.

"Of course I'll come over," Ellen said enthusiastically. "And give Raoul my very best regards this evening."

"You know," Sandy said as Ellen motioned to the waiter for their check. "I'm not going to worry about you anymore."

They parted outside the cafe and Ellen went off to the super market. She could hardly control the new vital force that pulsed through her veins. Every muscle in her body stretched and yearned as though coming awake after too long a sleep. She thought about her wardrobe and realized how dowdy it had become. Why must she continue to hide her slender curves and the fullness of her bosom? She could not deny the passions which lay inside her. They crouched with readiness. For three years she had mourned Warren's death. She had been faithful to his memory. But now her youthfulness had begun to rebel against death in life. She ate, she breathed, she slept. And her sexual passion could not be ignored any longer.

Ellen went into the most exclusive dress shop in town and purchased the clinging garment which would tell the world that she was once more ready for love.

Sundown shadowed the hills and still Warrie hadn't come home. Ellen tried not to hear the clock ticking and forced herself to refrain from glancing out the window. She went to the oven and took out the apple pie, happy to see the crust flaky and browned just right. This would be a good surprise for her son.

As Ellen was becoming frankly worried, she heard the screen door slam.

"That you, Warrie?" she called, trying to keep her voice cheerful.

"Who else?" Warrie said as he came sauntering into the kitchen. His baseball cap had streaks of mud and Ellen saw a tear in the sleeve of his new shirt. But she did not reprimand him.

"Guess what?" she said brightly.

"Yeah, what?"

Then she saw him sniff and a suspicious look brightened the hazel eyes which were so much like his father's. Tall for his nine years, he walked with his hands jammed deeply into his pockets. But for all his efforts, Warrie could not look tough. The inheritance of Ellen's tip-tilted nose assured him a baby face forever.

"Do I smell *cooking*?"

Ellen untied her apron and hung it on the wall hook. "You smell baking." She took down a couple of dishes and cut them each a slice, then spooned vanilla ice cream onto the plates.

"How about that!" Warrie said and pulled up a chair.

"Clean hands would make it taste better," Ellen ventured.

Warrie shook his head and pulled the cap further down over his eyes. "I'll take a fork," he said.

Ellen knew better than to make a point of washing up. She watched him bolt the pie, grateful that he enjoyed it. She wondered how far Warrie would cooperate with her new plans. Perhaps she didn't even deserve his help. Truthfully, she hadn't been very much of a mother to him. Always dependent upon her husband, Ellen didn't know the meaning of forcefulness or consistence. She needed guidance almost as much as her son. But now things were going to be different. She prayed that Warrie would make it possible for her to build a substantial homelife for them both.

"You know, Mom, you're a pretty good cook," Warrie said after finishing the second piece. He started to wipe his mouth on his sleeve and quickly, Ellen handed him a napkin.

"Really think so?"

"Sure, or I wouldn't be saying it, would I?"

His blunt honesty was on Ellen's side. "In that case," Ellen said, clearing the dishes, "what would you say to us having supper together a little more often?"

She watched him rock the chair back against the yellow wall paper. The delicate pink lips pressed together in a grim line of consideration.

"I guess that would be okay," he said. "If you don't try to fry bacon. You make the world's lousiest bacon."

"But you liked the pie."

"Yeah, that was fine."

Well, at least this was a beginning, Ellen thought. She felt encouraged because Warrie did not run out again to leave her alone. He stayed in the chair as she washed the dishes, kicking one sneakered foot thoughtfully against the crossbar.

"How'd things go in school today?" she said casually.

"Not bad. We only had a class for an hour. It won't get rough till tomorrow."

"You know, I met your new teacher when I brought in the books you asked me to return."

"So?"

"Well, I found him rather pleasant, that's all. He's not an old grouch like the one you had last year."

"I guess he's okay."

She could hardly expect Warrie to share her own enthusiasm. He wasn't the kind of boy who attached himself to people quickly. Yet she felt confident that Jay Masters could reach him. The process would be a slow one, of course. But the influence would be lasting. She wanted to talk about Jay Masters to give herself an excuse for thinking about him.

But Warrie had other things on his mind.

"I guess I might as well tell you now," he said abruptly.

Ellen recognized the tone in his voice. During the summer she had spent close to fifty dollars for broken fishing rods and lost baseball gloves. He had a way of destroying the possessions of others and making it seem like an accident. Ellen couldn't understand this because she bought Warrie everything he wanted. Her mind did not delve into the psychological factors of her son's behavior. She understood too well how much he missed his father. But she did not believe this sufficient cause for him to become a delinquent.

"What is it this time?" Ellen said with the gentle resignation that was her habit.

"Joey Probish's bicycle," Warrie said flatly. "He thinks I broke the chain."

"Did you?"

"I guess I did. It needed to be fixed anyway. But I was the last one to ride it before it came apart."

Fervently Ellen hoped that Jay Masters' camping group would put an end to this sort of thing. Already she felt as though she were depending on him.

"Mrs. Probish'll be calling you one of these days."

"You know, Warren, I'm getting awfully tired of apologizing for you."

"Don't bother," he said and left her suddenly alone in the kitchen.

Once again Ellen realized that she had not handled the situation properly. All her good intentions crumbled to nothing. She looked around the large kitchen feeling helpless and bewildered.

But she managed to gather her emotions and went to the telephone. She didn't know Mrs. Probish very well. They passed each other very occasionally in town and exchanged bright impersonal smiles. Ellen trusted that the woman would make it easy for her to pay the repair bill without fuss or explanation.

Ellen dialled the number and heard a deep richly melodious voice say hello. She hadn't realized that Mrs. Probish was quite so charming and when the woman invited Ellen over to clear the mishap away, she felt almost pleased to go.

Doctor and Mrs. Probish lived in a conservative two story house on the far end of town. Ellen pulled the car into the driveway knowing that the few dollars for Joey's bicycle would make very little difference in their financial affairs.

She rang the bell and heard slow chimes echo through the inside hallway. A few seconds later the door opened and Mrs. Probish took Ellen's hand and brought her cordially inside. Ellen's embarrassment dissolved beneath the lovely smile of this tall woman with blonde hair cut short to frame her beautiful head.

"You know I didn't really ask you over because of the boys," Mrs. Probish said.

She brought Ellen into the living room where a maid was just setting down a variety of canapes and crystal stemware filled with sherry. The high ceilinged room hushed the sounds of movement and added a classic touch of grace to the French provincial furniture.

"Thank you for being so kind," Ellen said, accepting a glass of the wine. The cushions of the sofa yielded just softly enough to her body so that she could sit at ease without being overwhelmed by them.

"In fact I'm glad that bicycle is finished once and for all. Joey fell in love with it and wore it down to the ground. But we couldn't convince him to get a new one. Your boy did us a favor, my dear."

"Just the same, I'd like…" She felt Mrs. Probish's glance touch the intimate points of her own body and Ellen uncrossed her legs to make certain that she wasn't sitting awkwardly.

"Of course I understand that you feel obligated." She sipped at her own glass. Ellen admired the natural color of the woman's lips. They were an extraordinary red without lipstick. Her face, completely free from cosmetics, had a soft luster of health just slightly tanned by the past summer.

"If you don't mind," the woman continued, "I'd like you to spend the money on a ticket to the benefit show Saturday evening. My husband is a great one for research foundations. I have one ticket left and I'd like very much if you would join us. We never see very much of you, Mrs. Tendler. I think this would be a fine opportunity to become a little better acquainted, don't you agree?"

Before Ellen could say yes or no, Mrs. Probish pressed the ticket into her palm and closed Ellen's fingers around it. Ellen felt complimented that this woman could be interested in her. She had a European polish which Ellen admired. The cut of her silk blouse was neat, almost austere. But beneath the soft material, firm breasts protruded with small delicate grace.

"I'll be happy to attend," Ellen said with sincerity. The woman seemed to cater to her in small ways that made Ellen feel important though she could hardly define the pleasant sensation. "I'm afraid I haven't been very social these past few years. But I think it's time to become interested in everything again."

Mrs. Probish set down her emptied glass and took up a short cigarette holder of ivory. "I'm so glad you decided to stop wasting yourself," she said. "How often I've seen you and thought what a pity it is for such an attractive person to hide herself away. You are attractive, you know."

Ellen felt her own glance flutter away from the blue eyes basking upon her. She was certainly accustomed to compliments. But for some reason, these words from Mrs. Probish embarrassed her. Perhaps it was because so much time had passed since words of approval had been part of Ellen's life. Or maybe it was because the older woman's serene face radiated an ageless beauty which Ellen's appearance could never match. Though she felt that Mrs. Probish's words were sincerely spoken, she wished that the doctor would come in and add a lighter touch to their conversation.

To break the silence which made Ellen feel awkward, she asked politely about Dr. Probish.

"Oh, Charles is very well, of course. You know these men who are devoted to research. They never have time to be anything else except well."

Ellen noted with curiosity the intimate tone coming into the woman's voice. She treated Ellen as if they were old friends. It was a flattering gesture. Undoubtedly, a friendship with Mrs. Probish could be very rewarding. Because she was a doctor's wife, this woman might understand better than most the difficulties that Ellen was beginning to face. Life had been fairly simple when she had been in mourning. But now, coming back into the world again, Ellen realized she had many problems which could not be readily solved. Mrs. Probish might be able to answer some of Ellen's questions. Help her gradually to adjust socially and physically. Ellen needed the strength of a woman wiser than herself. Sandy could help her laugh at her problems but Mrs. Probish might be able to help her to work them out.

"I'll be looking forward to Saturday evening," Ellen said, placing the sherry glass gently on the table.

"Yes, so will I," Mrs. Probish answered.

Ellen looked up into the lustrous eyes and felt a subtle strength flow toward her.

She left the house feeling glad that Warrie had given her a reason to know Mrs. Probish better.

As she drove home the night air perked thoughts one after another into Ellen's mind. During this one day, so many things had happened that she could hardly believe it was a day out of her own life. She felt strangely thrilled knowing that there was suddenly so much to look forward to. Usually one week followed the next in a frustrating pattern of sameness. But for once Ellen could not now predict what was going to happen. Tomorrow night Jay Masters would be spending the evening with her. Innocent though this seemed on the surface, she could not deny her response to this young man. He seemed to hold for Ellen a quiet but delectable secret, like a toy dangling just beyond her reach.

Perhaps they would share wonderful hours together. The bond of Warrie might draw them into a relationship close and precious. But she must remember to think of Jay Masters as a teacher. In time their own desires might grow beyond this toward more personal fulfillment.

Then on Friday night she would be stepping out like a young debutante, into the glittering gaiety of Sandy's world. Ellen felt sparkles of eagerness. She wanted to dance again, laugh again, be with people who knew how to have a good time. Perhaps releasing herself in this harmless social manner would also release some of the stores of energy which had grown so dangerously large these past three years.

And Raoul. Dear Raoul. He had always kissed her with a special tenderness. She remembered the way his hands had held her never too close. She had thought him a prude when she was very young. Now she wondered if perhaps Raoul had been afraid to allow his passions to go beyond the control of his rational mind. Possibly Raoul had something violent and animal to offer which Ellen had never suspected.

Beside the highway Ellen heard the hidden rustle of leaves in the darkness. For once she did not feel the surge of loneliness which came to her with the setting of the sun.

Mrs. Probish would be her friend. Ellen looked expectantly toward Saturday night also. Inevitably she knew that Mrs. Probish would draw out her own confidence. Unlike the other women she had known, this person made her feel important rather than a participant in the game of competition for the opposite sex. Ellen wondered if she would have remained in seclusion so painfully if she had had the friendship of so warm a person as Nita Probish.

And so three paths lay brightly before Ellen as she went to sleep that night. Paths that would take her away from the emptiness in to the experience of learning what richness she held ready to share.

CHAPTER TWO

WARRIE had already dressed and left for school by the time Ellen awoke. She had slept so peacefully that he had failed to disturb her with his morning preparations. Were it not for the sound of the vacuum cleaner, Ellen might have slept on until noon. But Doreen was not the kind of maid to be daunted by Ellen's laziness. She had a practical, determined way of getting things done which Ellen admired. She lay in bed listening to the high wheezing noise. She smiled and turned onto her back and stretched slowly from her ankles up the length of her ribs outward to the tips of her fingers. She tried to remember what sort of dream had left her so content with herself.

As she did every morning, Ellen turned now and nodded good morning to the photograph of Warren which stood on the telephone table beside the bed. Ordinarily her thoughts would return to some little incident in their lives together. To remember a moment shared with him was all the happiness she had been able to wrest from her existence. A miserable kind of happiness which did not help her to face the day with courage.

But Ellen knew that Warren was not the sort of man to wish that she worship at the altar of their past. He had been a go-getter. And he would want Ellen to seek out another, second happiness. She smiled gratefully at the picture and pushed the covers away from her body.

The transparent pink of her nightgown added a young rosiness to her skin. Ellen looked down, languidly considering the picture of herself. The curve of her belly was still tight and firm as though she had never known childbirth. Men could still find her desirable, she knew. And the ample breasts which had known the searching lips of a man still rose as though seeking once again the rough tenderness of desire.

Ellen brought her knees up and the gown slid along her thighs. Warren had always slept naked. Pajamas, he'd said, were an insult to marriage. But he had enjoyed slowly removing Ellen's nightdress. He had a way of taking it up so that his fingers were always in contact with her skin. The recollection of this made Ellen shiver. Quickly she got out of bed, knowing too well how her thoughts could get out of hand before she realized what had happened to her.

She had many things to accomplish before Jay Masters was due to arrive. First of all, she wanted a shampoo and to have her hair trimmed so that the brisk weather would not blow it all to pieces so quickly. Since it was the middle of the week, she might be able to get an appointment right away. After the beauty parlor, she wanted to buy a few notebooks to keep Warrie's lessons in order. Then she must purchase a bottle of light wine to go with dinner, if Mr. Masters would stay to join her.

Dashing into the shower, she ran the soaped cloth rapidly over her limbs. Her mind sped happily over the list of little things she wanted to accomplish this morning. Bundled in the terry cloth robe, Ellen went in search of Doreen. She wanted to cook dinner herself this evening. Make a tantalizing and lavish spread to lure Jay Masters to stay. Doreen was a no-nonsense cook. Meat and potatoes with a couple of plain vegetables on the side. Ellen liked Warrie to have this kind of a meal. But it wouldn't go with Chablis.

She buttoned into a wool dress, took a quick glance at the seams in her stockings, and left the bedroom. The mid-morning sun splashed brightly over the furniture and pointed out the tiny particles of dust that Doreen stirred up with her cleaning rag.

"I'd like you to do all the mirrors today," Ellen said. "And I'll take care of dinner."

Doreen nodded without either smile or annoyance. She was a dependable worker who had been with the family for over five years. But Ellen didn't know what the woman thought about if she thought about anything at all. Her blonde eyebrows and lashes made her face look fragile and inappropriate for the sturdy muscles that wielded cleaning implements with ceaseless energy. Ellen knew as little of the woman now as when she had first come to work for them. Or so it seemed to Ellen. She took for granted Doreen's honesty and her dependable loyalty because Ellen herself was an honest and loyal person. It always surprised her when people turned out to be underhanded.

She took her sportscoat from the hall closet and flung it over her shoulders.

"I'll be home around four, Doreen." Then Ellen swept out of the house, her thoughts pleasantly absorbed with all the little chores to be accomplished.

She had hardly taken six steps toward the car when Ellen heard a horn honk across the street. Instinctively she lifted her head in the direction of the sound. She saw Sandy's gray Cadillac. But Sandy was not sitting at the wheel. A gentleman in navy blue suit and Homburg tilted across his forehead smiled at her.

Holding her coat tightly so that it would not slip from her shoulders as she hurried, Ellen crossed the street with a beaming grin on her own face.

"Raoul," she said. But the usual platitudes about how marvelous he looked would not come to her lips. He seemed very different from the shy young man Ellen remembered. Success colored him with a new feeling of strength. He sat very straight and his blue eyes examined her with appreciation. Ellen couldn't help thinking that Raoul had learned more in New York than just the practice of law.

"I hope you don't mind that I've been waiting here for you." His voice had taken on a polished depth. "When Sandy told me you had accepted her invitation for tomorrow evening, I suddenly couldn't wait that long." His arm leaned on the edge of the car but his fingers made no movement to touch hers. Despite the eagerness in his voice, those hands seemed very controlled. His nails were well manicured and his white hands looked smooth as though accustomed to touching fine things. Ellen wondered if the women in New York had taught Raoul all he needed to know about himself.

"You should have come inside," Ellen said.

"Oh, I didn't want to barge in on you. I just thought I'd take this chance."

"Well I'm glad you did."

As Ellen came around to the other side of the car and got in, she couldn't help wondering what it was about Raoul that seemed to be luring her. She felt a strange pull to know more about him. The excitement, the promise of a hidden secret made Ellen alert and keen to discover.

"Am I lucky enough to have you all to myself this morning?" He shifted into gear and started the car slowly away from the direction of town.

"I'm afraid not," Ellen replied earnestly.

"But I can drive you wherever you want to go. I'd almost forgotten what a pleasure it is to sit behind the wheel of a car without having to stop every three seconds for a traffic light or a tie-up. You won't deny me the little pleasure of being your chauffeur?"

"I'd be delighted, if you have the time." She enjoyed playing this game with him. Not knowing where it would lead or even what it meant, Ellen could not resist the challenge of rediscovering this man. He treated her with an easy manner that dissolved the years and the people who had come between them. A more ordinary person would possibly offer her some kind of belated condolences for Warren. But Raoul treated her now as a woman rather than as a widow. She felt grateful to him for this.

At Ellen's direction, he swung the car around and took her to the beauty parlor. Then he took her inside and without any of the awkwardness that men usually feel in such places, inquired of the receptionist when Ellen would be ready.

She noted the sharpened glances of the various women in the salon and realized it would soon be all over town about herself and Raoul. But Ellen didn't care. She was certainly free to see whomever she chose. With casual unconcern, Ellen submitted herself to the hairdresser and the manicurist.

Happily Raoul met her afterwards and delivered Ellen from one store to the next. He carried packages and helped her to select an after dinner cordial. Not once did he seem curious about the guest she was obviously expecting for dinner. Perhaps Raoul took for granted that she entertained often. And Ellen felt no need to let him understand that she had kept herself in a form of exile all of these years.

At noontime he took her for a bite of lunch. While they sipped cocktails and waited for the entree, Ellen felt a great desire to ask him about his life in the city. Raoul's sure manner of behaving seemed to add inches to his height. Even the pale hair had taken on a new vibrance. She had never noticed before the deep widow's peak above the forehead. He combed his hair straight back so that the ridge of his eyebrows appeared to thrust forward with masculine aggression. Instinctively Ellen knew that if he kissed her, it would be intriguingly different from the self-conscious attempts in their childhood.

Raoul took out a cigarette case with his initials on it and flipped the lid open. "Have you learned to smoke yet?" he said with a good natured grin that emphasized the tear-drop dimple above his cheekbone.

"Oh yes," Ellen answered, taking a cigarette and waiting for him to light it. "One learns many things when …"

She had not meant to bring up the past. She did not wish for Raoul to discover the anxiousness in her heart. For Ellen, the past was not those years of being with Warren but of being without him. She would feel more comfortable if Raoul continued to believe that she was not desperately in need of physical release.

Raoul studied her for a moment, then changed the subject. "I learned a lot in New York too," he said.

"Like what?" Ellen grasped eagerly at this chance to draw him out.

Raoul moved the ashtray across the white tablecloth so that it would be closer to her reach.

"Oh like, how nice it is to live in the country," he laughed. "I have an apartment on the top floor of a sixteen story building but still, you can't really see the sky."

"Or maybe you don't have time to look."

She could imagine him late at night with a beautiful woman reclining on his sofa. Why should he gaze at the sky?

"Of course I don't have time," Raoul continued. "That's why I took a week to come back here. Had I known that I would be able to see you, I'd have come back much sooner, believe me."

Ellen did believe him. She knew that he felt there was something incomplete between them. And she shared this sensation which gave her an odd thrill. If they had a chance for privacy, Raoul would not feel shy about attempting once again the preliminaries of love making. Only this time, he would know how to go about it with authority. She could imagine his lips closing down on hers, allowing her no excuse to squirm free. Indeed, she would give herself to him gladly. Raoul was no stranger. He made her feel like a woman and that the expression of womanliness came most naturally in the act of making love. He had completely outgrown small town inhibitions. Undoubtedly sex to him was as common an occurrence as sipping the Martini he had just finished.

The only thing that disturbed Ellen was her own sexual starvation. People who were accustomed to satisfying their physical needs had a definite advantage over her. They could think clearly. The enormity of Ellen's desires seemed to blur her rational sense. She wondered if the instinct for self-preservation was strong enough to keep her from doing something that she might later regret.

The waiter brought out platters of tuna fish salad garnished with tiny scalloped radishes. Gladly Ellen applied her fork to the crisp leaves of lettuce. Her appetite for food had returned along with her renewed appetite for life. The sweet aroma of freshly baked pastries came to her nostrils as another waiter wheeled by a serving cart of apple turnovers and rum baba. She remembered yesterday's attempt with Warrie.

And Ellen recognized that she must never do anything that could possibly hurt the relationship between herself and her son.

When they had finished lunching, it was hardly two o'clock. Ellen had already completed her shopping chores thanks to Raoul's help. She had two hours free now to spend with complete attention to him. But where could they go? She certainly didn't want to invite him home with Doreen in complete possession of the household.

"We can take that drive now," Ellen suggested. "You can fill yourself up on the country and go back to New York a happy man."

The sky, bright without clouds, curved above them paling gently into the distant hills. Raoul drove without hurrying beyond the clusters of homes to the flat field bordered by patches of woodland.

"You know why I never managed to shoot a rabbit?" Raoul asked. "Because I purposely aimed away. Someday, if animals ever learn to shoot back, hunting licenses are not going to be in such demand."

Ellen knew where he was driving. Raoul's casual banter did not take her attention away from the path of the car. Years ago they used to cycle out this way to Frog's Pond. She remembered the feel of black perspiration on her palms from the rubber grips on the bicycle. And she remembered, too, the sensation of doing something wrong when they would go off by themselves. But nothing wrong had ever really happened. And although she was glad in her conscience, something else in her always came home disappointed.

But Raoul did not talk about those times. When he parked beside the dirt road that led uphill to the pond, Ellen got casually out as though they were making this trip for the first time.

The damp earthy odor recalled walking barefoot and snaring a curious lizard peeping out from beneath a brown twig. Ellen walked gingerly now, careful not to catch her stockings on a pro-truding branch.

They reached the pond that lay calm on the surface with a moss covered log lying very still near the water's edge. Somewhere a cricket chirped and Ellen felt very far from the usual things which occupied her. She watched Raoul pick up a pebble and toss it across the stillness. The wave of concentric circles seemed to widen out toward her. She wanted to take off her shoes and go barefoot again if only for a moment.

"Do you ever come here?" Raoul said. Somehow his voice did not break the silence, but rather became a part of the woods and the autumn.

"No," Ellen said. "I guess I'm not the kind to wander alone." She stopped her words abruptly but it was too late. She had, in that instant, completed the betrayal of herself. No words could cover the yearning which had sounded in her voice.

Raoul came up to her but he didn't put his hands on her shoulders, which was his usual preliminary to a kiss. He merely stood very close. The faint odor of his shaving lotion came to Ellen.

"You're not the kind of woman who should be alone," he said. "You're much too desirable."

She knew that he must have said this to dozens of women by now. Yet she could not believe that the words were not meant only for her. Ellen felt herself leaning toward him. Something drew her closer to his body. In that instant she did not care what might become of her tomorrow. Ellen knew only that she needed arms around her. Strong, knowing arms to hold her in tight secure warmth. She needed to let the fire inside her blaze freely up. Her lips parted and in that second, Raoul pulled her savagely to him.

His mouth parted her lips further and she felt the insisting point of his tongue search and find her own. The world disappeared for her in whirling darkness as she closed her eyes and allowed Raoul's mouth to caress the length of her throat. A violent shivering consumed her body. She could not remain standing. Beneath the probing of his fingers, her body became weaker and she yielded it to him. Beside her Raoul tore open the buttons of her dress and pressed his head between her breasts.

She needed him. More than anything in the world, she needed a man to use her. Her heart pounding wildly felt as if it had jarred out of place and was dancing down into her stomach. She needed to stretch her body wide and receive the answer to her own insisting need.

Her fingers went into Raoul's hair and grasped his head closer to her chest. She could feel her body growing beyond the confines of prim girdle and brassiere. Insanely she wanted to tear off all her clothes and lie naked here in this eternal setting.

A leaf caught in her hair and crumpled into tiny bits as her head thrust from side to side.

Then a strange thing happened which brought Ellen abruptly back to reality. She heard the ticking of Raoul's wrist watch as his hand went beneath her head. The door on her vault of self-preservation clicked suddenly shut, as she remembered that she had to be home in time to make things ready for Jay Masters.

Summoning a remnant of strength, she pushed Raoul away and turned quickly aside so that he could not pull her to him again. She knew that if she did not force herself to be aloof from him, the next instant would find her yielding completely to desire.

"Not now," she said hoarsely without daring to look at him. "I can't ... I mustn't."

She heard a breath escape him in a sigh of puzzlement. Ellen pulled herself completely free and stood up on trembling legs. With shaking hands, she brushed the dirt from her coat and tried to straighten her hair.

"Please try to understand," she said in a low voice. "I didn't mean to ..."

"That's all right," Raoul said. His voice was tight, the words clipped and sharp. "You don't have to explain. I know how you are, Ellen. For all that life has tried to teach you, you're still a scared little girl. I'm very sorry for you."

No, it wasn't that at all, Ellen tried to object. But she didn't have the strength to make him understand her situation. On the surface, it seemed that she had lured him on for the pleasure of denying him a final triumph. Baited by the longing inside her, propelled by the irresistible force that was growing daily further beyond her will.

If Raoul was bitter, there were no words to soothe the wound. Perhaps he had a right to accuse her of playing him for a fool. But that wasn't it at all. Everything had gotten somehow twisted up. And Ellen didn't know how to begin unravelling their predicament. Undermined by sheer physical frustration, she started back toward the road and the car. She must concentrate on Warrie and being a presentable mother to his teacher. Now of all times was no moment to be selfish.

Raoul helped her into the car and started on the road back. Once or twice she tried to explain to him. But it wasn't something Ellen could say in a few words. Nor did she want him to know about her problem with Warrie.

"Raoul," she said at last. "I want you to do me a favor."

"Certainly. We're not enemies, I hope."

"Will you give me another chance?" Her voice implored him to be patient with her. She didn't really know what she was doing except stumbling along a road of passion and hoping without reason that it would lead her to peace and fulfillment.

"Let's be honest, Ellen. I'm not a virgin anymore and neither are you. If two adults can't manage a friendly relationship without these adolescent fireworks, I'm not so sure it's worth the effort to persist. You know how many years I've wanted you."

He was driving faster and the wind smoothed the ruffled thinking. Ellen had no doubts about her desire to go to bed with Raoul. Truthfully her nerves were in such a condition that she would eagerly go to bed with any man who was healthy and discreet enough not to ruin her reputation.

"Can't you accept that this time was just the wrong time?" she said desperately.

"All right," he said. "We won't make a farce of this. I hope to see you at Sandy's home tomorrow night. Let's trust we enjoy ourselves. I'll forget about this afternoon and we'll begin all over."

"I promise it will be different," she murmured.

They rode the rest of the way to Ellen's house in a half strained silence which neither felt it necessary to break.

Ellen came inside and went straight for the bathroom. She didn't want Doreen to see her looking like such a mess and she hardly took time to drop the packages on the dining room table.

Alone with the full length mirror, she surveyed her creased and grass-stained coat. Where she had been and what she had done showed obviously all over. Her hair was completely tangled and bits of leaves still caught in it. How many people had seen her riding down the street with Raoul and looking like this?

Ellen stripped off her things and brushed her hair vigorously. For Jay Masters she had to look calm and untroubled. No decent mother runs off to the woods with a man not her husband. And yet what are women supposed to do who have known the caresses of marriage, have become accustomed to them and suddenly are bereft? If one could turn off the body as one turns off a faucet, how simple existence would be!

Perhaps if she were living in a large city, the ebb and flow of events would have settled the matter for her long before the matter had become so urgent. Ellen had never lived in a place like New York. The few times she had been to visit left her with the impression that people could solve anything because there was always someone to whom one could turn. Masses of people meant to Ellen a greater possibility of making friends. Not until Warren's death had she learned the meaning of having to keep her own counsel. She did not enjoy this kind of secrecy.

She needed but a few minutes to clear away the outward signs of her experiment with Raoul. But the recollection continued to trouble her. She remembered not alone in her mind, but most vividly in her flesh. Unpacified, her nerves refused to be subjugated. She had to put her lipstick on twice before she could brush on an even outline. Her skin felt as though the little invisible hairs were standing on end. She felt irritable and close to tears.

For a long time she stayed at the bathroom sink, bathing her wrists in tepid water. She dared not think about Raoul and how he would greet her tomorrow evening. Perhaps she would be wiser not to attend the party altogether. But that wouldn't be fair. If she had humiliated Raoul, he deserved a chance to reinstate himself.

Ellen downed a couple of aspirin tablets and went out to see if Doreen was ready to leave for the day. Ellen wanted to be alone with her trouble. She had to learn that complications were not unusual for a person who lived a normal life. Her seclusion for these past years had weakened her. She knew very little except the passive occupation of indulging her memories. She must strengthen herself so that minor incidents would not incapacitate her.

Wearing a silk housecoat, Ellen went into the kitchen to start preparations for dinner. Perhaps Warrie would come in shortly with another tale of his day's exploits. She needed patience and understanding for him. Surely being so concerned with herself could not help her son. Working slowly, she dressed the chicken and put it into the oven.

No doubt Jay Masters would appreciate a home cooked meal. He didn't look like the sort of man who was accustomed to eating dry sandwiches and soup. She wondered if he had a family and where they lived.

Doreen came into the kitchen. "I guess that's everythin' for today."

Ellen wiped her hands and paid the girl. "Thank you, Doreen," she said. "I hope you have a nice weekend."

"The same to you." She adjusted the old fashioned hat so that its limp feathers straggled down over her heavy bun.

Ellen was in the habit of giving the woman her old clothes, which Doreen managed to fix so that they fit her. She never complained about the lack of money or a wayward husband. Doreen might be a contented person in her own dogged way. She certainly would hold up better than Ellen if her husband died.

Returning to the pan of Hollandaise sauce, Ellen tried to concentrate on the dinner. She hoped Warrie still had an appetite by the time he came home.

She took out the silver dinner service and placed settings for three on the large table. Ellen knew it was almost hopeless to think that Warrie would want to join them. But she wanted to give him the chance.

The occupation began to settle Ellen's nerves as she concerned herself with how the evening would go off. With napkins and glasses in place, she went to the bedroom and selected one of her new silk dresses. The pale orange color added a glow to her skin which made her look carefree in an elegant way. She buckled the wide belt snugly, emphasizing the narrowness of her waist and the curves above and below it. A crystal necklace high on her throat, shot sparkles of color in a way that framed her face and led the eye upward over the heartshaped chin to the dark gray eyes. A touch of dark blue mascara made her eyes appear large and penetrating. She enjoyed applying the cosmetics as though she were painting a new personality over her face.

Warrie came in as she was applying cologne to the inside of her forearms. He strode to the door of her bedroom and stopped short at the threshold. His baseball bat, shouldered like a gun, grazed the molding.

"You look different," he said. "Where's Doreen?"

For some reason Ellen had expected him not to take the change so lightly. She felt both disappointed and relieved. At least she wouldn't have to go into a long explanation to suit him.

"Doreen went home. It's way past six o'clock, you know."

"I didn't eat supper yet. Did you eat supper?" He slid the bat off his shoulder and let it roll on the carpet.

"No. I thought we might have supper together."

"But we did that last night."

"We don't have to do it if you'd rather not. I asked Mr. Masters to join us tonight. I thought it would be nice if the three of us could eat together."

Warrie looked at her with eyes wide and stricken. He wet his lips, then pursed them in an expression of fantastic anger.

"Why did you have to go and do a thing like that?"

Ellen had expected this reaction. She picked up the bat and handed it back to him.

"Well I told you last night that I think he's a nice man. He's a regular guy. Like your father."

She knew the comparison would cut Warrie deeply. But she knew, also, that the time had come for both of them to stop worshipping at the altar of a memory. They stood in danger of forfeiting the rest of their lives unless they learned to accept Warren's death as a natural happening. Summoning all her confidence, Ellen smiled at the boy and touched his perspired head with her lips.

"I think Mr. Masters wants to talk to you about something you might like."

Warrie stood rigidly beside the molding, his nostrils flaring as though he were confronting an enemy. "He's got nothing to say that I want to hear." Overwhelmed with hate and confusion, he clutched the bat fiercely.

"That's up to you," Ellen said. "If you don't want to join us, you can have dinner wherever you like. But after all, you're the man of the house and I'd miss not having you with us."

Ellen's floundering words failed to reach their mark. Warrie felt that she had betrayed him. As lost and helpless as her son, Ellen went to the mirror and tried to appreciate the image of herself.

"You're terrible," Warrie said. The syllables came out slow and heavy and unforgiving.

She heard him fling the bat against the wall and the plaster made a thin echoing sound. In a moment he had slammed out of the house again and Ellen prayed that he would not get himself into trouble.

Perhaps a more competent mother could run after her son, get him by the ear and drag him back inside for a good healthy beating. She had never laid a finger on Warrie. She believed that floggings could breed only hatred. Ellen remembered the one thrashing she had gotten in her life when her father had caught her exchanging curiosities with an older girl in the garage. She had not believed that the other girl had hair in the place she bragged about and Ellen wanted to see for herself. The childish episode had grown into an example of wickedness. And it had taken her a long time to confide in her father after that.

Ellen hoped that Warrie would never feel he could not tell her something for fear of being hit. The question of how to punish him without alienating his confidence left Ellen defeated.

When Jay Masters arrived promptly at seven, Ellen had managed to pull herself together into a respectable appearance. She saw he carried a briefcase and took it from him as he came into the foyer. He allowed Ellen to do this with an ease that assured her of his friendliness. No formality of teacher and parent produced a barrier between them. She wished Warrie could appreciate this as much as she did.

"I met your boy down the road," he said. "Apparently I'm expected by all." His wry smile absolved Ellen from all explanation.

"Well, you didn't think he would welcome me with hugs and kisses, did you?"

"I don't understand why not." Her fingertips were chill and she felt no appetite at all for dinner.

"If Warren would accept anybody with a full heart, he wouldn't be suffering from his particular problem, Mrs. Tendler. Nor would I be here this evening to help you work it out."

"Yes, of course." Ellen led him into the dining room. "I hope you'll excuse me for being so intense. You see, I mentioned his father. Apparently it was the worst thing I could have done."

"I think that depends a good deal on what it was that you said."

Ellen felt her throat tighten with embarrassment. She could hardly quote her words without indicating something to Jay Masters she'd rather he didn't know.

"Won't you make yourself comfortable? Dinner is almost ready."

He pulled out a chair and sat down on it sideways. His action made it seem as though he were in the habit of dropping by for a meal any time.

"Aren't you going to tell me?" He determined not to accept her evasion.

Ellen clasped her fingers together as though holding on to herself. For the good of her son, she would have to be completely honest with this man.

"I told you Warrie you were a regular guy. Just like his father."

She waited for something to explode or fizzle. But Jay Masters simply listened without any perceivable change crossing his eyes or his mouth.

"That's a pretty rough thing to tell a hero worshipper about his hero."

"I suppose Warrie and I suffer from the same trouble."

Ellen had never dreamed that she could speak this freely to a person she had just me. She felt as though social discretions did not exist. Only truth and this need for the facing of truth concerned Jay.

"If it's any help, let me assure you that I believe Warren will come around much sooner than seems possible at this time. A child who spits things out is a lot easier to get to, than one who keeps things hidden."

Ellen knew that she did not have to voice the tremendous thank you which radiated from the center of her being. She felt it blossoming on her face in the form of a relieved smile.

"I hope you're ready for dinner," she said.

"Oh yes," he answered. "I'm glad you went to the trouble."

Ellen brought the many dishes out from the kitchen and with a sense of gratification, watched him eat. She tried to follow his example but the food wouldn't go down smoothly. Tactfully he ignored her lack of heartiness and applied himself with energy sufficient for them both.

"I guess you knew that I would be partial to home cooking," he said between mouthfuls. "Had a devil of a time in the service."

Without rushing and with the utmost in table manners, he consumed enough for three men. His huge frame seemed to absorb the food and turn it into muscle. Any woman would find it a pleasure to cook for him. Temporarily Ellen put away the problem of her son as she allowed Jay to enjoy himself.

"Bet you were your mother's favorite son," Ellen commented as she gave him the dessert dish.

"Not at all. My mother farmed me out when I was seven. Too many kids in the family, all of them just as voracious as myself. So I was my aunt's favorite son. Maybe because I was her only son." He laughed heartily and Ellen realized that this contented man must have come a long way from heartbreak. No wonder he enjoyed being with children and doing his utmost to help them. Ellen could not imagine a mother turning one of her own children out of the house. But she herself had never known poverty. And not having enough to eat was something Ellen held in awe. What would she do about Warrie if she had to work for a living? In some ways, life had conspired to protect her. Perhaps some day she would learn what to do to deserve this.

Without asking permission, Jay helped her clear the dishes. The action came so naturally that Ellen did not think to discourage him. If she had to face all of the truth about herself, she might as well begin by realizing how much she enjoyed the company of this man. They could talk about stocks and Wall Street and he would make her feel at home in the conversation.

Irresistibly her mind began to wander with the thought of having Jay alone with her in the dark. Would he take her savagely as Raoul had tried? If he took her hand and led her into the bedroom, she would go with him because he would make it seem the most natural action in the world.

"Now if you'd like," he said, "we can take a look at the arithmetic lessons."

"I bought some notebooks this afternoon," Ellen volunteered. "If I left it to Warrie, things wouldn't be in much of an order."

She felt a little more sure of herself as she saw Jay nod with approval.

He took out some slim volumes with his briefcase and they sat down side by side on the sofa in the living room.

The nearness of him made Ellen force herself to concentrate on the work. He crossed his legs at the ankle, propping the book on his knee. She saw the shape of his ankle bone beneath its brown woolen sock. Did he take his clothes to a Laundromat? Surely he couldn't afford a maid on his teacher's salary.

"I think if you can do half a lesson a night, we'll be doing well. You'd better start with single column addition."

She could tell that he was concentrating on the work and not on her dress or the perfume. Was her appearance wasted on him? No man, no matter how earnest, could be immune to the attractions of a woman. Perhaps he just couldn't think of her that way. In his mind she might be just another parent of a problem child. But they were almost the same age. And he knew she lived alone.

Could it be that Jay had a mistress or a girl he was in love with? If that were the case, she would have known it by now. A word, a hint, some sign of interest somewhere. She was convinced that Jay had no woman he really cared about.

Ellen leaned closer over his arm as Jay wrote samples of the work for her. Her arm brushed against his hand, but she saw that he paid no attention to the accident.

In twenty minutes he had everything outlined for her. "I'm not so foolish as to think you'll be able to get Warren to do all of this," he smiled. "At least not at first. But try what you can without getting into a battle with him. I'm sure it will come along better and better."

Regretfully she saw him get up and snap the lock shut briefcase. She didn't want to be left alone. At least just yet. Warrie was out on the loose doing only God know what kind of mischief. The idea of lingering over what had happened with Raoul threatened to consume her if she were left to her own thoughts. Jay seemed to have a key to the bright side of things. She needed that key badly.

"Another cup of coffee before you go?" she said. Ellen did not bother to disguise her need of his company. He wanted the truth. She would give it to him.

To her surprise Jay said, "Why not?"

Ellen got two clean cups and filled them. "You know," she said, "I'm half afraid to discover what he's been doing outside all this time."

Jay stirred a teaspoon of sugar, then set the bowl gently on the table. "He won't do anything drastic. You might not realize it, Mrs. Tendler, but your boy is a very curiosity ridden youngster. You told him I had something to say to him. He's not going to wander too far afield before he finds out just what it is I have on my mind."

"How do you know I told him?"

"Because he told me."

They both laughed and Ellen felt ten pounds lighter in her head.

"That's better," Jay said. "Maybe if you learn to have more fun, your son will get the idea that things aren't so terrible after all."

"I'm beginning to know that," Ellen said. "I really am."

Jay got up and buttoned his jacket. "Then everything will be fine."

There was no other way she could detain him without making a nuisance of herself. Ellen saw him to the door with sporting acceptance of this fact.

"I'll phone you tomorrow and check how things are going."

"You know how grateful I am."

He stepped outside and a cool draft blew in, pressing the thin material of her dress close against her thighs. But his glance did not take advantage of this accidental display.

Ellen closed the door, then went to the window to watch him stride out of sight.

Ellen felt a little better in her spirit. Because of Jay, she was convinced that all was not hopeless concerning Warrie. Jay would phone tomorrow. He would phone or drop by a few times next week. Maybe with time, he would grow to like her for herself, separate from the challenge of Warrie. She did not consider herself very well versed in the art of seduction. But her liking for Jay would show her how to get to him. At least he was placing himself within her reach. She wouldn't have to chase him out in the open where people could see and talk so that it might get back to her boy.

Or maybe she was so blind and so anxious that she did not recognize Jay's approach to her. He was well versed in the art of tact and gradual success. His very profession groomed him in the ways of slow accomplishment. She must learn to accept the methods and ways of his personality. If she could muster the patience.

Jay Masters was apparently a man who wouldn't care for women to take the aggressive role. The way he conducted himself in her home showed Ellen how much he preferred the old-fashioned conduct. She would have to wait until he got around to doing something more positive himself. But there must be a way in which she could help speed the process up a little.

She went into the bedroom and took off her dress. Unhooking the bra, she examined the ridges the elastic had made beneath the soft flesh of her breasts. She could imagine his large hands massaging them with tenderness and growing passion. As she thought of this, a chill ran down the line of her stomach. Ellen fell down onto the bed and shut her eyes very tight. She didn't want to think about sex. How horrible to become a slave to something which ran wild without either thought or consideration. But she could not battle herself free. A twitching began very small and tremulous on the inside of her thighs. She brought her legs tightly together and held them stiffly quiet.

If Warrie came in now, how could she talk to him? She must get out of the house. Go for a walk. Look for the boy. that would not leave her alone to these thoughts. flung herself off the bed and into a pair of flannel Slacks. Tomorrow night she would be able to release some of this emotion. Ellen promised herself to dance with many men. She would not spend the evening alone and intensely with Raoul. She would accept the offers of all the men who found her amusing or desirable. Sandy would be her guide. She must learn to joke about her desperation and relieve it in thousands of tiny ways. But only one way really beckoned to her.

Dressed in a cardigan sweater, the slacks and a pair of loafers, Ellen looked hardly more than sixteen. She sent herself out of the house only to discover that Warrie was sitting beside the front gate.

"What are you doing here?" she said, startled by the nearness of his presence.

"Nothing."

"It's getting late. Don't you think you'd better be getting ready for bed?"

"I don't guess you care what I do."

For a moment Ellen could find no answer to this accusation. Nothing, of course, could have been farther from the truth. She sat down beside him on the grass. "Why do you say that?"

"Why shouldn't I?"

"Because it isn't so. That's why." Exasperated and frightened of herself, puzzled and concerned about the boy, Ellen could no longer contain herself. She put her arms around him and hugged the small body close. "Don't you know I love you? I don't care about anybody or anything else in the world, except you." She kissed him fiercely on the cheek trying to give him the huge package of her love.

Her lips found a wet trickle on his skin.

"Well, you sure don't show it!" He tore himself from her arms and ran into the house.

Ellen remained alone in the darkness. She pulled her knees up and rested her forehead against them, fighting to understand how such a rift could have dug its way so widely between Warrie and herself. Had she really done the wrong thing by asking Jay to dinner? She couldn't believe that Warrie resented the man with such ferocity. They'd known each other so short a time. Three or four days at the most. No, it wasn't Jay's fault at all. Her own stupid, blundering expression concerning Jay and Warren. But how could she undo the damage?

Trying to listen to herself think, Ellen heard the sound of tree frogs, cricket-like above her. She tilted her head skyward and saw herself tiny beneath the millions of stars spilled across the high blackness. Somehow there must be an answer to all this misery that followed her child. For herself, she could not really care anymore. At least she was old enough to understand her own longing. But how could Warrie cope with the invisible weight burdening him?

In her desperation Ellen mentally put the problem into Jay's hands. He seemed so sure that Warrie could be straightened out. She must have faith in Jay's certainty. He knew children. Warrie could hardly be the first of his problems.

She could no longer think about it. Her mind was going in circles, furious and blurred. The wisest action would be to go inside, see that her son got to bed, and try to get some sleep for herself.

She came into the house and discovered that Warrie's door was shut. Ellen knocked gently.

"Would you like a glass of milk?" she asked.

"Go away," came in a muffled sound. He had buried his face in the pillow and didn't want to see her.

"Good night, my dear."

Ellen went to her own room and took off her clothes.

Sleep evaded her. She lay on her back wondering how her body could have the nerve to insist at a time like this. Sex was the least of her concerns right now. Yet it clawed inside her, screaming for attention. Her eyelids would not remain closed. She stared out the window at the silver treetops. Once upon a time there was Warren beside her. She could almost feel his breath against her ear. If he were here right now, he would say, "Don't worry, honey" and all the conflicts would cease in her mind because Warren said so.

Don't worry, honey. They were the last words on his lips as she held his hand in the hospital. Three short years ago and Warren was kissing the tip of her nose with laughter that turned quickly to flame. Sex had been an unused word then. Love, only love united their bodies in an expression of everlasting faith and adoration. Warren, with the little boy's lips that could bring her alive into a searing point of ecstasy.

She hadn't known a day's worry when Warren was with her. He would take her up into the mountains where the snow glared in fantastic whiteness beneath the sun's eye. And at night they would sit beside the fire drinking something warm and humming to the off-key ukelele that he packed along on every trip. Oh those nights, when the wind rattled the windows but could not disturb the love they shared beneath the heavy blankets.

Winter and summer, all the seasons melted into one long dream of holiday when Warren came to hold her on his lap. And after their child was born, the family became even closer. He bought his son presents for the time when he would be old enough to go skin diving. They talked about college for little Warrie and maybe a sister to join him.

And then, just as it happens in the newspapers. Just as it happens to someone else, but never to you, Warren's car skidded on a small lake of ice hidden in the shadow of a tree.

To remember these things now was unbearable. Shouldering responsibilities was the one thing Ellen had never been taught to do.

She got out of bed and went for the bottle of Scotch in in the living room cabinet.

As she poured herself a drink, Ellen remembered the promise to herself that she would not do this anymore. And she had tried. She really had tried. But would it be better for her to spend a night fighting off the horrors of her helplessness? She would not be fit to cope with Warrie in the morning if she spent the night entirely without sleep. The whiskey went down her throat raw and distasteful. She was not meant to be an alcoholic. All of her felt revolted by the need to escape this way. In a quick succession of swallows, she downed half a water glass of whiskey, then returned to her bed.

Now she shut her eyes and deliberately started to count slowly backward from one hundred. Her mind became woozy and she felt the muscles of her calves beginning to relax. She waited for release into dreams, believing that a nightmare, anything would be better than wakeful thrashing. Inhibitions of consciousness dropped slowly from her. Her thoughts danced around Raoul and Jay and tanned men lying on a beach. She was the only woman amongst them and all eyes were focused on her red bathing suit. One by one she seduced the men. Eagerly, happily she accepted them into her arms and held them close until the moment of their climax.

The wishfulness of her subconscious mind gave Ellen a shabby duplicate of satisfaction. But mercifully, she did not remember these dreams when she awoke in the morning.

CHAPTER THREE

ONSIDERING what had happened last night, Ellen wondered if she dare leave Warrie alone tonight. For the sake of her own health she had to get out among people. If she did not believe this completely, she would have called Sandy right away and begged off from the party. Instead she went about the business of getting through the morning and the afternoon, carefully avoiding thoughts about her son.

Occasionally she glanced at the telephone, knowing that she could not possibly expect it to ring until three o'clock. She imagined Jay sitting at his desk or writing at the blackboard, involved with the responsibility of two dozen children. What did Jay do when doubts assailed him?

The sunless sky melted morning into afternoon without any change either toward rain or toward brightness. Vivid colors of the countryside beyond her windows now partook of the grayness, subdued into dull waiting. Ellen snapped on the television set, but the commercially cheerful voices jarred on her nerves.

When the phone rang at last, Ellen rushed to it without pretense of being called away from other occupations. The voice that spoke to her belonged to Nita Probish.

Would Ellen do her a tremendous favor? Charles would be detained tomorrow because of an emergency operation. She would be very grateful if Ellen could call and take her to the theatre.

Yes, of course. She'd be happy to.

Ellen replaced the receiver, wishing she could spend the rest of the day with Nita Probish. She wanted to hear about far away places and people. Take her mind off herself. If Jay would only call, she'd be free to hop in the car and visit with Mrs. Probish right now.

In her imagination Ellen tried to call the woman by her first name. Nita. A wave of self consciousness rolled over Ellen as she pronounced the syllables. Far more comfortable to say Mrs. Probish. But the woman said Ellen and referred to her own husband by his given name. Ellen was not sure why she felt so formal about Mrs. Probish. A vague feeling of safety reposed in the use of surnames. A sensation of closeness, almost of touching when she spoke the name Nita made her return to the safety of Mrs. Probish. It was silly to make such a fuss about nothing. She would just have to get used to it.

When the phone rang again, Ellen had already started to get dressed for the evening. She picked up the extension in her bedroom and leaned against the wall. Her skin, still damp from the after-bath lotion, felt cool and resilient. The sensation of vitality in her limbs added a new lilt to her voice.

She told Jay about the episode with Warrie and he replied will all the comforting words she had expected from him. Jay was becoming for her an emotional reservoir. She drew on him for strength, for assurance, for optimism. And he gave these to her with generosity. After Ellen hung up, she felt renewed. Warrie would be occupied this evening with Jay. The two of them were going to arrange about camping supplies for the first outing this weekend.

Ellen wondered what magic of words Jay used to smooth things out so that Warrie would be cooperative. But she didn't dwell on this. The relief of knowing that her son was in good hands sufficed to free her mind. She could go out tonight and really enjoy herself.

She slipped into the new cocktail dress of green brocade and worked to pull the zipper which ran the length of her back.

The material flared in the rear and fit tightly in sheath fashion along the front of her body. She enjoyed the feeling of being discreetly covered but just as discreetly displayed. One of the tricks of appearing desirable was, to Ellen's way of thinking, an ability to have it appear accidental. She walked a few steps toward her mirror, watching how the cloth moved with the breathing of her diaphragm and swayed with the flexing and unflexing of her thighs. Raoul would appreciate this dress. Ellen felt that it didn't look small town.

From her dressing table Ellen took out the box of jewelry which had lain there for so long unused. Delicate pearl earrings that dropped the length of her jaw bone were the only ornaments she decided to wear. Fearful of appearing overdressed and therefore over anxious, Ellen settled for a black velvet coat and clutch purse to match. She examined the total effect and decided that Nita would approve of her taste. Nita who automatically wore and did the proper things was subtly becoming Ellen's criterion.

Humming a little melody, Ellen locked the door and went to her automobile. She could smell the fragrance of her own perfume and it put her in a nonchalant mood. Ellen turned the radio dial until it reached some dance music. She knew that her feet remembered how to dance. How would it feel to be held in the arms of a well-dressed man and circle with him around the floor? Sandy's home had parquet floors, smooth and lovely for dancing.

Ellen found a parking space, took one last glance at herself in the rearview mirror and went up the steps to Sandy's door. The night, very dark without stars or moon, sent a winter chill through Ellen's coat.

She pressed the bell and waited. The sound of music and voices came through the door. Ellen was glad that she was not the first one to arrive. She preferred to come in when the party was already in full swing. This would prevent any words of serious greeting between herself and Raoul.

"Ellen, baby. Come in." Sandy put a heavy hand on Ellen's shoulder and kissed her on both cheeks. The alcohol on her breath had a fresh astringence. Sandy most probably had made an effort not to drink anything all day so that she could get grandly drunk in Raoul's honor.

Ellen allowed her coat to be removed and glanced at the dozen faces chatting in various corners of the gold and black living room. She recognized most of the people. They were known as the Trading Post set. Warren and she had never made close friends among this group. They had in common the so-called modern ideas about marriage and neither she nor Warren had cared to participate in the trading of husbands and wives which comprised most of their evening activity. Ellen knew that Sandy did not much care for the idea either. But she had little ability to tie down her husband.

She looked around the room for Raoul and discovered him on the bay window seat listening to an animated description of something that had to do with giraffes. He seemed rather engrossed in the movements of the brunette's neck.

But Henry dug his way out of a smoky cluster and swooped down upon Ellen. He was a big man in all directions and his pink skin glowed as smooth as the floor. Nothing had ever hurt Henry or taken his mind off himself.

"Good to see you." He handed Ellen a tall glass of something with Shweppes. "Don't know how you managed to hold out this long." He winked and taking her by the wrist, brought Ellen over to the group of people he had left.

She went through the motions of saying hello and allowing herself to be told that she hadn't gained an ounce or lost a curve. Frankly the men inspected the curves of her body. If they had not approved, Ellen might have been embarrassed. But Ellen wanted admiration now to make her feel a part of things. Admiration meant acceptance and more invitations and the opening of life beyond the doors of her own household. Jonny Dake, who had inherited a fleet of trucks from his father, reached out and patted Ellen on the hip. Unconsciously she moved away from his touch. Then, realizing that it looked unfriendly, she stepped an inch closer to him and laughed from somewhere deep in her throat.

As she stood surrounded and encouraged to finish her drink so she could have a refill, she heard Raoul's voice.

"I didn't hear you come in," he said, taking a cigarette from between his lips and dropping it into someone's abandoned glass.

"Yes, I know," Ellen said. "You were busy."

She nodded in the direction of the brunette and found that she now had Jonny captive on the windowsill. The gold drapes made a perfect frame for her ample physique. Ellen wondered how Sandy's love of sunshine could withstand all this closeness and tension.

But Sandy was rattling ice cubes at the buffet table. Her flesh forced out the material of her dress in excess rolls beneath the line of her brassiere. She was getting to look more and more like her husband.

"How about a little something to go with that drink?" Raoul said. He appeared very much in control of himself and not at all a part of this gathering. But, of course, Raoul didn't need illicit entertainment to stave off the boredom of small town living.

"Yes," Ellen said. "I didn't have much supper."

"I hope you aren't worrying about something?"

She had no desire to tell Raoul about Warrie. "Just dieting," Ellen laughed.

She followed Raoul to the table and waited as he helped Sandy mix another batch of drinks. Little brother fixes everything, Ellen thought. She wondered if Sandy felt ashamed of herself in contrast with her brother's success.

"Here you go," Raoul said, returning with a plate of cold cuts.

"Aren't you going to join me?"

"I'm happy with this." He lifted the highball and took a small sip.

Ellen felt sure that he would not take another drink during the rest of the evening. The antics of these people gathered to honor him made Raoul feel like a murderer among kiddies playing at cops and robbers. Ellen could see that none of the group impressed or interested him. He had seen and done it all before.

Ellen ate the cold cuts in an effort to prevent herself from getting high. Wherever she turned, someone handed her another drink. She knew she was downing them too fast.

"Let's go sit someplace," she said.

But Henry had set a pile of records on the machine and the brunette came over to ask Ellen's assistance in a harem dance. Helplessly she watched the mirth spread over Raoul's face. He relieved her of the plate and glass. "Go on, Ellen," he said. "It's all in fun."

Why not? Ellen thought. She wasn't any better than these people. Maybe a lot worse because they did in the open what she dreamt of in secret.

The brunette got her into the middle of the floor and motioned the men to make a circle around them. They moved forward eagerly and began clapping in time to the music.

Ellen followed the leader and as she whirled, the shining eyes of the men seated cross legged on the floor became a blur of animalism urging Ellen on. Some weak sense of decorum tried to control Ellen. But this lasted for only a moment. She felt very happy. Nonsensically happy. The life of the party. Free. Young. Willing.

"Go on, kid." Henry's voice spun in her ear.

Flinging away all sense of confinement, she gyrated her shoulders and belly and knees, outdoing the brunette who was now doing the giraffe dance with her long white neck.

Only the end of the record put an end to Ellen's movements. A film of perspiration made her feel less prim. The motor of her heart churned. She went back to Raoul and gulped the rest of her drink.

"Another," she said and found herself being fondled and joked with by three men whom she had hardly said hello to during the past three years.

Sandy came over and pulled them away from her. "Let the girl breathe." She laughed, but a vein of seriousness ran through her words.

"She can breathe very well," Michael said. Michael was handsome in a long-lashed and violet-eyed way. He had just married his fourth wife. Ellen recalled reading about it in the paper and feeling sorry for the girl who believed that Michael could be forever faithful to her.

"Why don't we try that again," Michael said. "I'll be one of the harem girls this time."

"You and me both," Henry said.

"Oh please," Sandy groaned, staring in mock horror at her husband's protruding stomach.

But Ellen was enjoying the nonsense. She felt very wanted. And she liked the sensation. Men. Disgusting, desirable. She prayed that Warren, wherever he was, would forgive her for this thought.

The brunette was holding Jonny Dake by the corners of his bow tie and showing him the movements of the dance. With each step, he moved closer to her until their bodies came in contact.

"Supposing we cool you off a little bit outside," Raoul whispered. He slipped his fingers around her wrist and led her firmly away from the group of her admirers.

They reached a low oriental table and he motioned for Ellen to sit down on it.

"I didn't know you had such a capacity to enjoy yourself," he said. A hint of sour amusement tilted his lips upward in a pussy cat smile that made Ellen defiant.

"Of course," she answered unsteadily. "I always have a good time wherever I go." The flame was burning high inside her and she wanted to lie down. If only there was a swimming pool so she could strip off her clothes and swim naked and feel cold water washing over her breasts.

"Good. I was honestly worried about you, you know."

The blare of rhumba drums from the second record made their conversation private despite all the people.

"No one has to worry about Ellen Tendler," she said. "Don't you know that rich young women are the most fortunate beings alive? They can do what they want, when they want and not give a hang about tomorrow. God protects drunkards and wealthy females."

"And that's why I specialize in divorce law."

She was sick of hearing him sound so smart and above everything. Time was when Raoul couldn't open a door for a woman without tripping over his own shoes. Now he was Mr. Know It All. She didn't need him. Any man in this house would be willing to take her home and stop on the way for a get-together session. But she knew that Raoul wasn't chasing after her with the same kind of hidden desire. He would take her or leave her as she wished. Yesterday's humiliation was not Raoul's, but her own exclusively.

"I like you," Ellen said. "Did you know that you're very wicked and that's why I like you?"

She could hear the thickness in her own speech. But she didn't feel drunk. She merely felt released as though suddenly she had the courage to say and do all the things that lurked behind her everyday politeness. It was true what she had said about being fortunate. Supposing she did go to bed with Raoul? Who could stop her or do her harm afterward. Everything seemed amazingly clear and simple to her now. She wondered where all the problems had gone.

The brunette came over and sat down on the table beside Ellen. One strap of her gown had slipped off her shoulder but she didn't seem to notice.

"It's getting wild out there," she said without enjoyment. "Why is it that men always get wild when ladies want to be ladies?

It must be nice in the jungle where nobody can pull your clothes off because you aren't wearing any."

Ellen realized why the girl looked so familiar and so unfamiliar at the same time. She had submitted to a nose job. That part of her face looked like an oasis of piquancy in the midst of drooping sadness.

"You're Gloria Drew," Ellen said without caring that the sentence sounded ridiculous.

"I am Mrs. Michael Rancher," she answered with exaggerated pride.

"Congratulations," Raoul said softly.

He made no pretence about wanting to be alone with Ellen. This was the first time Ellen had seen him exhibit rude manners and she felt startled, flattered and upset.

"You're not a nice man," Mrs. Rancher said.

"That's true," Raoul answered, as though brushing off a fly. "I don't have many friends."

Ellen could not bear to have the conversation go on like this. It was ruining her lovely evening.

"Michael is a very handsome man," she said, hoping that it sounded like a particular compliment to Gloria.

"Both handsome and intelligent," Raoul offered, making a game of the conversation.

The sound of glass shattering diverted their attention. Jonny had knocked over one of the Chinese lamps and was down on hands and knees trying to scoop the pieces together.

"You'll cut yourself," Sandy cautioned. "Wait till I get the sweeper."

The music played on as all the men converged to help Jonny. With caricatured slowness they dropped bits of the lamp into ashtrays, glasses and empty vases.

"Who's going to dance barefoot?" Michael shouted. "A gold piece for whoever dances barefoot with me!" He pulled off his shoes and socks.

Gloria ran over and dragged him away from the danger zone.

"Why do they go to all this trouble?" Raoul said to Ellen.

She sat very still, not wanting to make any more bright repartee. Very simply she wanted to be alone with one man. A man who would marry her and be interested with her in all the plain activities that would never make the gossip columns. If she could understand this new, darker side of Raoul, she could even consider living with him.

But perhaps he didn't care for the idea of marriage any more. If the women in New York spoiled him, why should he care to settle down with one person? Surely his youthful love for her was not enough incentive. What did he really think of her now anyway? She couldn't tell how much he liked her. She wondered if yesterday's incident nagged at him.

"Why don't we go someplace where I can clear my head?" Ellen said softly.

"Certainly."

She could not detect any eagerness in his voice. Raoul was beyond the stage of licking his lips for a woman. Maybe she wouldn't be adequate for him?

They walked around the edge of the group still clearing up smithereens. Without protest, she followed him upstairs. A deep carpet muffled the sound of her heels. She didn't care if the people looked around and suddenly wondered where they had disappeared to. Raoul was the guest of honor. He should be present until the last person left. But if the guest of honor chose to go away first, who was she to deny him that privilege?

He took her into one of the bedrooms. The darkened outlines of furniture swept Ellen's desire beyond the confines of good sense. Anyway she had abandoned good sense when she had entered that dance with Gloria. Now she expected Raoul to drag her down on the bed and take what she wanted so desperately to give him.

She stood waiting. But he opened the doors of the terrace and led her out onto it. The shadows did not hide her disappointment.

Raoul lit two cigarettes and gave one of them to Ellen.

"What did you want?" he said as she leaned over the railing clenching her fingers around the wood furiously. She did not feel the cold air drying her overheated skin. The passion inside her could be cooled only by a man's arms, his lips, his possession.

"Who said I wanted anything?" Ellen retorted.

"Now be sensible, little girl. We couldn't possibly enjoy ourselves if someone came running in in the middle. Perhaps you don't think it's important to me that we hit it off right. But it is."

Important to him? Could he stand there and honestly say that one more sexual act in his life was important to him? Her anger began to subside.

But when, she wanted to ask. How much longer could she wait without going mad? If he suspected the strength of her desire, he would not treat their situation so lightly. But she had purposely led him to believe that sex wasn't so desperately important to her. So she could not blame him for taking his time. Raoul knew how to handle situations. She must respect his judgment.

He came up behind her and cupped his hands around her waist. "I do want you," he said. "Much more than anyone or anything. I've wanted you and dreamed about you through all these years. In a crazy way, you might say I've been faithful to you. I thought that yesterday it would be perfect between us. I still think it can be. But not if we have to rush like two criminals."

Childishly the thought went through her head that Raoul would be in town only until Sunday. She took a deep breath of the night air and tried to pull all the pieces of herself together. She turned and put her head against his cheek. She felt his hands move upward and mold themselves around her breasts. She put her own hands on his and pressed them harder against her.

"I'm sorry," she murmured. "I don't know how this got so complicated."

"Blame it on the atmosphere," Raoul said. "If I had remembered what Sandy's parties were like, I wouldn't have consented to being in the middle of one. So let me apologize to you, Ellen."

Gradually he worked her downward into a more sober mood. But although her mind came back to its proper place, her body still lurched wildly with unsated longings.

"Perhaps you'd better take me home," she said. If they could be together and alone in the car, they could find a place somewhere to expand the extent of their intimacy. Ellen promised herself that tonight she was not going home to do battle again with her frustrations. Intently her mind focused on the goal of possessing this man who would not judge her for yielding her body.

Though Ellen did not realize it, she did not want any of the men in Sandy's group. The idea of going to bed with a married person revolted her sensibilities. If Warren were alive but impotent, she would go gladly into eternity without satisfying her longings.

They returned to the party and no one made any comment about their disappearance. Of course nobody cared. Subdued now with alcohol, they sat around telling each other pornographic stories which seemed the last outpost of titillation.

Ellen said a quiet good-bye to Sandy while Raoul went to get her coat.

"You'd better drive," she said as they approached the car.

She gave him the keys and settled back against the leather seat. Her limbs, played out with nervous energy, fell limp. She couldn't drive if she wanted to.

"We don't have to go home right away," she said as he brought the car onto the roadway. Icy winds whipped at her hair and she felt it rise and spill without care.

"Where would you like to go?"

"Oh, any place. But not home just yet. Let's go for a ride in the country."

"Isn't it too cold for you with the top down?" He sounded so confoundedly sensible.

"Well then stop and put the top up."

He brought the car to the side of the road and brought the canvas cover into place.

"Cozier this way," he commented afterward.

Ellen sighed and moved closer to him. Irresistibly her hand moved to his knee. The material of his trousers, fine wool, felt good to her touch.

"Isn't there a motel around on one of these roads?" she asked.

"Sure. There are lots. But who within a radius of thirty miles doesn't know us?"

Of course he was right again. She didn't care if they went back to Frog Pond. Even the back of the car would do. Anyplace.

Languidly she lifted her hand and turned on the radio. A muted trumpet solo played to them. She put her head on his shoulder. Her hand, as though it had a life of its own, moved inside his jacket and caressed the muscles of his chest. "You must look beautiful naked," she said.

"No doubt," he chuckled. "Why don't you light me a cigarette?"

"You smoke too much." She felt in his pockets for the lighter, taking time to explore parts of his body. She wanted to rip the white starched shirt off him and bite into the skin.

Quietly she lit him a cigarette and placed it between his lips. "If you weren't smoking, I could kiss you."

"Wait till we park."

His words encouraged her to patience. The speedometer needle wavered around thirty five. He could go faster without exceeding the speed limit. Why didn't he?

"A little way up there's an old detour."

"I know," Raoul answered.

Clinging to him, she decided not to say another word until he stopped the car. What was the use of all this conversation? She didn't want to talk or make sense. Or do anything except...

She felt the automobile slow, then bump off onto the dirt road. He pulled onto the grass and drew up the brake.

Ellen held her breath as he grabbed her and dug his teeth into her lips. She wanted him to abuse her. Maul her. Tear out the thing that was eating away at her soul. She felt the steering wheel jammed against her arm but it did not matter. He dragged off her coat and she felt something on her dress tear. That did not matter either.

His hands moved beneath her slip. She felt the touch of his fingers on the margin of her flesh between stockings and girdle. She wore no panties, but the girdle itself was a deadly chaperone. The elastic material held her thighs firmly together. She wanted to spread her legs so Raoul could search more intimately.

"Unhook them," she whispered.

She waited, quivering, while he fumbled with the garter hooks. Then she felt the sudden sag of her stockings. Released, the girdle began to shimmy upward along her hips. A cold wave of air licked at her, sending goose pimples along the creases of her skin. She felt his palm, now, cupping her and she rubbed against it nervously. Her own hand groped for the zipper on his trousers.

She felt that special part of him harden to her touch. To Ellen it was more a dream than a reality that she was so close to fulfillment. She moved her hands along the warm flesh, savoringly.

"Oh, how I need it," she said, not realizing that her thoughts came out in audible words.

Somehow his hands had found and opened her brassiere. Her breasts slipped out from beneath the satin supports. All her clothes were askew. Her body was a chaos of desire.

"Hurry," she moaned.

Anticipating the moment, her hips began to move in the motions of intercourse.

"We'd better get into the back seat," he said harshly.

Panting, she did not want him to let go of her. Not even for the moment it took to change seats.

"No, please," she gasped. "I can't wait."

"Don't be ridiculous," he said cruelly, but she did not catch the tone in his voice.

He dragged her out of the car and pushed her into the rear seat. She did not need room to sprawl. Holding him tightly on top of her, she struggled to get her underthings off so that he could reach her. They fell off the seat and squeezed together on the narrowness of the floor. Wriggling upward along him, she tried to adjust their bodies for better contact. Ellen felt nothing of the discomfort. She knew only the need for ultimate fulfillment.

But Raoul pushed himself away and crawled back onto the seat. "This is impossible," he rasped. "We can't. Not like this."

"Yes we can!" Her voice was louder, more desperate than she knew.

"Be quiet. You'll wake up ..."

"There's nobody to hear us." She clawed at his collar, trying to bring him down onto her again.

"I said no, Ellen."

Her body went suddenly cold. "You're a fool. A miserable, wretched fool." The words were aimed at herself.

"Why don't you come with me to New York?" he said. "It'll be so simple, so much more pleasant. And we can spend the whole night together, as though we were entitled to enjoy ourselves."

Convulsed with trembling, Ellen twisted away. She heard sobs tear out of her throat though the last thing in the world she wanted was to cry.

"Take me home," she said. "I never want to see you again."

Raoul leaned back against the cushion and let a long sigh escape him. "You don't understand," he said. "You just don't understand."

There was nothing to understand, Ellen thought. Now at the moment of showdown, he had rejected her. She had come to him with every inch of her ready for his possession. And he had thrust her from him. She felt as though her body would burst wide open and splatter her insides all over the universe. She couldn't go on like this. It was inhuman.

"I am a fool," Raoul said. "I'm everything you want to call me." His voice sounded flat and defeated.

"Please take me home."

"All right. But no matter what you do, I'm going to see you again. Make it up to you. I won't let you slip away from me, Ellen. I must sound crazy to talk this way."

Slowly Ellen lifted herself and slid up onto the seat beside him. Her mind was very clear with a super clarity that she remembered experiencing in times of extreme illness.

"No," she said in a very low voice. "You don't sound crazy, Raoul. Just mean and sadistic." She didn't realize what she had said or whether the words were actually true. But she felt, now, that Raoul was exacting his own peculiar form of revenge. Sandy must have told him that she never went out or diverted herself socially. Undoubtedly Raoul knew how much her body craved release. So he was playing a game with her. Tantalizing her to the very pinnacle of desire, then withdrawing the promise of fulfillment.

"Will you take me home or shall I walk?" Her words were sharp as her thinking. She got out of the car, adjusted her clothes and returned to the front seat. "Or better still," she said. "I'll drive you home first."

With Raoul still in the back seat, she turned the key in the ignition and headed the car back in the direction of Sandy's house.

Ellen dropped him off and started immediately back to her own place. The clock on the dashboard said two and she knew it was fifteen minutes slow. She hoped that Warrie had gone directly to sleep after reading the note she had left for him. What a relief it would be to return to the safety of her own bedroom. She was no match for Raoul's intelligence and subtlety. Sex was something she had looked forward to as a simple joy. She had never realized it could be a weapon with which one person tortured another. The full horror of this understanding made her almost nauseous.

Was this the hidden something about Raoul which had intrigued her? She could not believe that he had turned into such a creature. But perhaps he was not completely to blame. Her rejection of him years ago might have started the process. And yesterday could have completed it. If she had given in to him at the pond, would their relationship be different now?

She must stop thinking about Raoul. If she allowed him to come near her again, there was no predicting what might happen. Her lower lip felt very sore and she flicked her tongue over the area. The skin had begun to swell. Thank heaven it was such a dark night and so late. How could she explain this appearance to anyone? Even Warrie would be able to tell that something had happened to her. She must look as if she had been raped. Ellen laughed bitterly to herself.

The car headlights picked out the familiar lane to her house and she slowed the car in so as not to wake Warrie. She decided not to pull into the garage. She'd make much less noise if she parked in the drive.

Gingerly she turned the key in the lock and found that the front door was open. One thing she had managed to teach Warrie was never to leave the door open.

Curiously she stepped inside and saw the shadow of lamplight slanting out from the living room. Was he sitting up then? waiting for her?

She came inside and looked squarely into the sleep filled face of Jay Masters. Ellen's hand went to her mouth.

"Hello," Jay said, suppressing a yawn. "I hope I didn't frighten you."

A panicky feeling took hold of Ellen. What would he think of her coming in at this hour, looking the way she must look. There was no mistaking what she had been through.

"Warren and I came back here in a specially good humor this evening," he said. "We read your note together. Then we played a few games of rummy."

"You don't have to explain," Ellen said.

"But I want to. This must seem like a terrible imposition." He rolled down the sleeves of his shirt and straightened the knot of his tie.

"Not at all, Jay. I know it wasn't a good idea to leave Warrie alone in the first place."

"On the contrary. It was a splendid idea. Honestly, I didn't have anything to do tonight and your place is so comfortable. I guess I just availed myself of the surroundings. Then before I knew it—asleep."

Ellen remained in the shadows of the foyer so that he could not get a closer look at her. She was grateful that sleep still squinted in his eyes.

"I'll be going now."

"Would you care for some coffee before you leave?" She really wanted him to go away immediately but she could not treat him like a stranger.

"Thanks, but don't bother. It is late. And I know you must be very tired."

Ellen couldn't argue with that.

He buttoned on his jacket. "You should go out more often." He smiled gently. He came up to shake her hand good night. She could not evade him and she saw his eyes narrow with concern as they focused on her mouth.

"Did you fall?" he said.

She knew the liquor on her breath could not escape her nostrils.

Helplessly she watched his glance inspect the rest of her.

"For heaven's sake, Ellen, what happened to you?"

Not Mrs. Tendler. Ellen.

The honest concern in his voice, without discretion, without a thought that she had a reason to be ashamed of herself for what had happened to her. Jay stood waiting for an answer.

Ellen knew she couldn't lie to him. But how could she tell him the truth?

"Please don't ask me," she implored. "Maybe someday. But not now. I'm very tired."

"Well, put some iodine on that bruise. Will it be all right if I stop by tomorrow morning?"

"Yes, of course. I'll be glad to see you then."

He ran his fingers worriedly through his hair. "Don't forget to use that iodine," he said and closed the door quietly behind him.

Ellen collapsed onto the sofa. Her pose with Jay was finished. No matter what she told him, no matter what excuse she invented, he must realize what she had done this evening. And if she lied to him, he would understand that she was lying. But how could she expose her very soul to a man of his nature? What did he know of frustrated desire? To him, a mother of one of his pupils was just that, not a woman too. She was a sexless thing with only one duty. If he knew what thoughts wracked her mind and pursued her at night, would he not consider her unfit to raise Warrie?

And yet, for Warrie's sake, perhaps it would be better for Jay to know her for what she really was. Torn between her desire to do everything possible for her son and the desire to preserve herself in the eyes of this man whom she admired, Ellen lay motionless, unable to work out the predicament which confronted her. Her body seemed to float away from the earth, escaping the impasse of reality. In the weird shadows of the room, she prayed for some greater knowledge to come to her aid. Only once before had she seriously turned to God for intervention. And then it had not been for herself, but for her husband.

But no voice came to guide Ellen out of her trouble. Tomorrow Jay would come, expecting her to confide in him. Why did he take her so for granted? She had a right to her own private life. But if she made this evident to him, would he not withdraw his help from Warrie in the belief that Ellen was not sincere?

Her mind worked furiously, though no movement of her body indicated that Ellen was awake. The more she thought, the more tangled her problem became.

She could refuse to see him. Yes, that was it. When he came tomorrow, she could plead illness. He would understand or pretend to understand.

The hours fled swiftly and soon the first sounds of dawn came in through the opened window. How glad the birds sounded, greeting the new day. Ellen wished that time would stand still until the end of time. She pulled herself off the sofa and the ache in her legs was unbearable.

She could not face the reflection of herself in the mirror. Her usual habit of taking a drink to put herself to sleep would not work now. The thought of liquor revolted her. She searched in the medicine cabinet for sleeping pills and found an old bottle with three of them left inside. She pulled them onto her palm and swallowed them all with a bit of water.

Hardly aware of her action, she dropped her coat onto the bedroom chair and let the rest of her clothes slide to the floor. Then she crawled into bed and waited for the pills to take her into oblivion.

A laggard drugged sleep seeped into her body. As she sank into a morass of dreamlessness, she knew that she could not possibly be awake when Jay called.

Ellen opened her eyes, feeling as though only a second had passed since her last waking memory. The covers lay too heavily on her perspiring body. She did not feel at all refreshed but neither did she feel frantic and cornered.

The sound of a ball being bounced came to her hearing.

"Warrie?" she called. Though she put effort into the word, her voice did not come out loud enough to carry to the other rooms. "Warrie?"

"You finally up?" he yelled back at her, the ball still bouncing. She did not have a headache but her skull felt much too large for her body. Turning her eyes to the square enamel clock on the dresser, she saw that it was after one. But she didn't feel very much like getting out of bed. Her hot body lay weakly buried beneath the covers. Gingerly she touched her lip and gratefully realized that it had not gotten any worse.

It didn't feel like one o'clock. The room was too dark. She heard an irregular tinkling sound against the window pane and watched droplets slide along the glass. So that was why Warrie had not gone out.

Ellen pulled herself out of bed and wandered over to the mirror. She had to face herself now and see what signs of damage remained. Except for the lip, there was nothing unusual about her appearance that a bath and make-up wouldn't fix. Even lipstick would cover the swelling nicely. The tiny crack had already begun to knit, making a slender brown line. She pushed back her hair and felt the dryness in her mouth. There was something that she had to remember that she couldn't.

Swallowing, she felt the beginning of soreness in her throat. She needed a vacation from herself. A couple of weeks on a nice warm island where she could lie on a hammock and look out to a calm sea. Yes, it was a beautiful thought.

Ellen heard Warrie's footsteps getting closer. "Ready or not, here I come," he said.

"Will you wait a minute?" she called.

"Ready or not."

She grabbed at the kimono hanging on the closet door and managed to get it over her as Warrie burst into the room.

"You're a lazy one," he said pleasantly. He seemed in command of a satisfying bit of knowledge. His face was clean for a change and dark patches of water stained his hair where it was neatly combed. "I've been up since eight o'clock," he announced.

"Why?" Ellen said, feeling her head slowly shrinking to the right size.

"You know why. Mr. Masters tells you practically everything."

"But he didn't tell me this, darling."

"Good." Warrie maneuvered the ball into the pocket of his jeans. "I won't tell you either."

She felt glad that Warrie shared a secret with Jay. Especially if it had this uplifting effect on him.

"And you know something else? Mr. Masters was here this morning and you were snoring like a horse." The thought tickled Warrie and he began to laugh. "Yeah, just like old Seabisquit."

"I suppose you brought him in to listen," Ellen said, horrified at the thought that Warrie might very possibly have done so.

"Nope. We made breakfast and then he went away again."

Warrie's unusually happy state gave Ellen a little lift. She put aside her own discomfort and found that her own lips were smiling, though somewhat painfully.

"I could use a cup of coffee," she said. "If you want to make it for me."

He looked at her with a second's suspicion.

"Yes, make me some coffee, please. You're dressed and I'm not."

"All right," he said, rising to the challenge. "I will so."

Well, at least now she had some further time to consider how to face Jay. Perhaps if she stalled long enough, last night's encounter would be forgotten. Or, at any rate, dropped. The solution eased her nerves. She went to the bathroom, splashed water on her face, then donned slacks and sweater. As long as Warrie was feeling so playful, she would play with him. Maybe they could read together. Or if she was really clever, get him to do some of the arithmetic problems. This was a perfect afternoon for it.

Ellen went into the kitchen and stared at the dozens of dishes strewn over the cupboards, the table and piled precariously in the sink.

"And what did you two people have for breakfast?" she said in a hushed voice.

"Scrambled eggs and coffee. What'd you think?"

Ellen didn't know exactly what she thought. Certainly not eggs. She couldn't imagine what flight of creativity had inspired the use of a colander, a cream sauce boat and the lazy Susan. But she thought it the better part of wisdom not to ask.

"Ready for your coffee?" Warrie asked.

She looked at the high flame licking up around the edges of the percolator.

"Ready or not," she smiled.

The continuing rain gave Ellen a feeling of coziness as Warrie's assistance made it increasingly difficult to clear up the kitchen mayhem. But she got the job done after a fashion and then she asked him to teach her how to play rummy.

He seemed a wealth of patience and happiness as Ellen concentrated on losing game after game to him. Only when she mentioned the subject of schoolwork did he balk. Well, it was too good to believe that he would give in on this point. Ellen tried to reason with him, but he insisted that she was spoiling their fun. Wisely, she dropped the subject.

"Did you mind very much that I went out last night?" Ellen said, not sure that she should talk about this either.

Warrie didn't answer right away. He bent over and untied his shoelaces. Then he tied the lace of one shoe to the lace of the other and hopped to the wing chair and fell into it.

"No, I don't mind," he said.

"Well, would you mind if I went out again tonight? I bought a ticket from Joey's mother…"

"Well, that's all right," he interrupted her with triumph. "'Cause I'm going out tonight too. So there."

Yes, the camping trip, Ellen remembered. But how could they go in this weather? Even if the rain stopped by nightfall, the ground would be much too sodden for sleeping.

"Where are you going?" Ellen inquired earnestly.

Warrie pulled his ankles apart so that the knot slipped open. "Do women always have to know everything?" The twinkle in his eye satisfied Ellen that he wasn't annoyed with her.

"I told you where I'll be. It's only fair now for you to tell me."

He thought this over for a minute.

"Mr. Masters got a whole gang of tickets for the basketball game. We're going to stay over at the Y and hike back tomorrow if the weather's nice. I need for you to say yes. And I'll need a little money."

Well, Ellen thought. Jay Masters certainly knew how not to disappoint children. She wondered how many other mothers were as glad as herself to say yes and spend a few dollars to be relieved of their youngsters for one night.

"He's got Frank's bus all set to leave at four thirty."

"Wonderful," Ellen said sincerely. "I'm sure you'll have a grand time."

"So you can go out any time you want to go out," Warrie said finally.

It was past four o'clock now. Ellen became increasingly aware of the difficulty she had in swallowing. She left Warrie and went to get herself a couple of aspirins. What she had taken to be after sleep sluggishness was rapidly turning into a cold in her system. She felt very warm beneath the surface of her skin.

The sound of rattling metal and the grind of gears thrown into neutral sent Warrie to the window.

"They're here," he said and dashed off for his old lumber jacket.

Ellen looked between the curtains and saw the ancient yellow bus packed with boys, whistling and jostling each other. For a moment she felt sorry for Jay surrounded by all this youthful vigor. But then she remembered that he loved every minute of it. He wasn't the type to bother with anything that didn't give him pleasure. She saw him climb out of the bus and run to the door. Ellen opened it as he reached the porch.

"Hi," he said, stepping inside and shaking the water from his hat brim. "Did Warren tell you where we're headed?"

"Yes," she said. "I hope you had enough to eat this morning?"

"Oh don't worry about that. I come from a long line of French chefs."

"So I gather," Ellen chuckled.

"Are you ..."

"Feeling much better this morning, thank you."

"Okay, I'm ready," Warren yelled at he came dashing out between them.

"Have a good time everybody," Ellen waved.

She watched Jay hoist Warrie up the steps of the bus and stood at the door until it rattled out of view.

Now Ellen had the whole long night to herself. She intended to enjoy the company of Mrs. Probish, Nita, and her friends. If only her throat didn't get any worse.

CHAPTER FOUR

Using Warren's large umbrella for protection, Ellen dashed the short distance to her car. The heavy downpour splashed her ankles and chilled her fet through the open-toed shoes. She turned on the windshield wipers and the heater, trying to disregard the aching which gnawed at all the joints in her body. Thick sheets of water made the headlights almost useless and she drove slowly through the fog of rain. The pounding of water on the canvas top irritated Ellen and made her feel closed in and trapped.

She arrived at Nita Probish's house tired and strained as though she had inched her way half across the world. But despite all this, she had an underlying eagerness.

Nita Probish opened the door and Ellen saw that she had not yet begun to get dressed for the evening. Her body looked very young in corduroy slacks with not a spare inch on her slender hips.

"Am I too early?" Ellen said.

"No. I'm glad you're here." She took the umbrella, dropped it into the stand near the door, then helped Ellen off with her raincoat. "Charles has been gone all day and Joey left with the group. In fact I was going to phone you and ask if you would come over early."

The sleeves of her shirt were rolled up past the elbow and Ellen admired the sleek sheen of her forearms. They had an almost translucent shine. Ellen wondered if her whole body were this smooth.

"I'll make us some tea, then we can chat while I dress."

If there had been any formality in their first meeting, it was completely dissolved now. The pounding rain outside made Ellen very glad to be in the warm presence of this person. She felt welcome and appreciated.

"Wonder how that old bus is doing," Ellen said as she took the cup Nita handed her and followed the woman into the bedroom.

"Let's not think about that," Nita said. "Seems to me you concern yourself too much with your role of being a mother."

She said the words half jokingly, but Ellen responded with a need to defend herself. Privately she had to admit Warrie was the center and totality of her life. She had no outside interests, nothing to make her selfsufficient. Perhaps she was embarrassed because this woman seemed to understand so much about her and Ellen could fathom so very little in return.

"I guess I'm over-anxious," she said. Ellen wondered if Mrs. Probish would be any different if she did not have a husband. To be part of a complete family could make one's outlook and interests broader and less fraught with overconcern.

Ellen glanced up from the study of her thoughts and found Nita Probish looking at her.

"I know that wasn't the right thing to say, Ellen. Forgive me."

Ellen tried to smile and pass the remark off as if it hadn't really hit her.

"You see," Nita continued, "Charles is away so much of the time that I don't even feel as though I have a husband. And Joey, well he's not exactly the apron string type. When a woman has so very little to do around the house, either she finds other, more constructive interests, or she gets herself into a rut."

She set her cup down on the dressing table and began to unbutton her shirt.

Still, Ellen thought, you have a man to make love to you at night. This was a great difference that Nita was not taking into consideration.

Instead of going behind the screen, Nita proceeded to undress within Ellen's view. Sipping at the tea, which felt soothing to her sore throat, Ellen watched the woman's movements. The body being slowly revealed to her showed none of the ravages of child-birth. The stomach muscles were tight as a young athlete's. The small breasts gave no sign of having nursed a child.

Ellen could appreciate this body objectively. She felt no inclination to look away. And since Nita herself did not require privacy, Ellen took for granted that she was at liberty to admire the female loveliness before her.

"I must admit," Ellen said, "you don't show any of the signs of being a conventional mother."

Nita had begun to massage the back of her neck. "Thank heaven," she murmured, smiling up at Ellen from the bent angle of her head.

Ellen was too curious to let the matter drop. She was beginning to wonder if Nita actually disliked being a wife and mother. She didn't give any signs of being discontent. Her home was managed with care. No scandal ever touched her name. But what did Nita really think, behind this well-groomed exterior? What did she want out of life?

"If I were you," Ellen blurted, "I'd be very thankful to have a home that runs so smoothly. You may not appreciate it, but I envy you. And I'd like to bet that lots of other women in this town would agree with me." A testy note had crept into her voice.

"Envy me?" She came over and stood before Ellen, her naked-ness exuding a hint of perfume recalling the mountain heather. "But why should anyone envy me, of all people?" She knelt and rested her palms on Ellen's knee. "Do I seem like a happy buffoon who has everything and thinks about nothing?"

"That's not what I meant." The conversation had somehow become very confused. Ellen thought she had stated her case rather clearly. Why did Nita misunderstand her meaning?

She wished Nita would get up from that silly position. She felt uncomfortable having this woman so close to her and without any clothes on. This being oblivious to one's body was something she did not understand.

"Look," Ellen said. "Do you know what it is to go to sleep night after night in an empty bed?" Exasperation was making her bold. She could not accept that a woman so fortunate as Nita Probish was not aware of her good luck.

"All right," Nita said. She got up with a sigh and took the cover off a large porcelain bowl labeled bath salts. "You're trying to tell me that I'm not lonely. That I have all the basic essentials in life to make any woman happy. But what you don't seem to understand is that not everybody likes steak."

Now Ellen felt completely lost in their conversation. By Nita's tone of voice, she knew that there was great significance in her last statement. Yet Ellen could not fathom what she was supposed to glean from it.

"No," Ellen said slowly. "Not everybody likes steak. I'm not sure that I care for it either."

"Oh?"

"Maybe I don't interpret you correctly," Ellen said.

Nita took a tremendous Turkish towel from the bottom drawer of the bureau and went with it to the bathroom. Ellen watched her lean over and turn on the faucets in the tub. Neither of them spoke now as the sound of water hitting the tub filled the room.

She saw Nita step carefully into the tub and slowly lower her body. Nita did not bother to close the door. She lay back and allowed the steaming water to lap over her breasts.

"Think about it," Nita said, picking up a bar of soap, "before you commit yourself any further."

Annoyed with herself for being so dull, Ellen did think about it as Nita's attention concentrated on the lathering of her arm and chest. Was it possible that the woman didn't love her husband?

Could she be playing the role of the happy housewife because she had no choice? But this wasn't the Middle Ages. If she didn't get on with her husband, she could certainly get a divorce. Apparently Joey would not stand in her way to this. No, Ellen could not make any sense out of Nita's cryptic remark. She would just have to go along until the woman's meaning became clearer.

She went to the dressing table and sat down before the ornate mirror. Crystal decanters of perfume reflected light backward from the glass. The whole room had a feeling of being removed from the ordinariness of everyday essentials. The white cushions on the several small chairs were hardly designed for practical living, but not one spot marred any of them. Only Nita's small watch, lying beside the nail buffer, indicated that this place belonged on the span from life to death. Otherwise this was a room devoted, in a hypnotic way, to the pleasures of becoming beautiful. But if not beautiful for her husband Charles, then for whom?

If Nita Probish were a man chaser, she certainly managed to keep it well hidden from common knowledge.

"If you want anything, cigarettes, anything, just make yourself at home," Nita called.

"Thank you," Ellen said automatically. Her preoccupation with the unravelling of Nita's strange conversation had made her oblivious to herself. Now, looking in the mirror, she saw that her eyes were too bright and the sensation of warmth beneath her skin had increased. A slight flush added color to her cheeks even beneath the rouge. She looked very alert and full of a verve that she was far from feeling.

Ellen turned away from her own image and saw Nita drawing the towel briskly along her back. She stood wet and glistening. Droplets of water slid along her ribs.

"Perhaps women envy you," Ellen said frankly, "because you don't have to work at the business of being attractive."

Nita's movement with the towel slowed. She stroked a damp lock of hair away from her forehead. The water on her lashes made of them a thick, curling fringe which emphasized the clearness of her eyes.

"No, you're wrong," Nita said, bringing the towel around the front of her and working it down from her throat. "Nobody envies me. Not even you."

Ellen wanted to protest but realized that it would sound ridiculous. She had never before felt inspired to argue with another woman about her appearance. Nor had Ellen ever been concerned with such a thing. Women had always been to her, well, just women. If she considered them at all, it was to compare them with herself. But she knew that she wasn't feeling any kind of competition with Nita Probish. It would be like comparing apples with peaches. Nita was a creature unto herself. She certainly had all the usual attributes of a woman. But she had something extra, too. Some vague quality which made Ellen defensive and slightly on edge. She wanted to show off for Nita. The idea felt childish but she could not deny that it was present. What was it about this woman that made Ellen want to shine and say all the right things and be approved of?

"Will you please bring me that large puff?" Nita said. "The one in the blue container."

Obediently Ellen brought the puff into the bathroom. Nita turned her back.

"If you'll be kind enough. I can't reach all the way down my back and since tonight is a special occasion..."

Ellen could see no reason why she should not oblige. Lightly she patted Nita's back, dusting the powder generously over the skin, which was indeed as smooth as the arms.

Despite herself the physical contact was beginning to stir something within Ellen. She wanted to touch that skin, not with the puff but with her own hands. She wanted to feel that smoothness for herself and be convinced that it was really as soft as she imagined. She managed to control the impulse. But the effort cost her the ability to make casual banter. She hoped that Nita would not become aware of her awkwardness.

At last Nita turned and took the puff from her. Ellen stood with her hands like gross pieces of wood at her sides.

"Thank you," Nita said. "It will take me just a moment to dress and then we can be on our way."

The statement relieved Ellen. Something very peculiar was beginning to blossom inside her. She must have a temperature, she thought. Perhaps she shouldn't have come out at all tonight.

As she was thinking this, Nita became suddenly impersonal with a relaxing charm that set Ellen's mind a little bit more at rest.

She spoke to Ellen about her childhood in Spain and how she had met Charles on a stormy boat trip across the Channel. Her descriptions of Europe delighted Ellen. She could almost hear the high whining sound of the Italian sirocco and taste the salty fish and chips wrapped in newspaper.

By the time they were ready to leave, Ellen was laughing happily and gave no more thought to whether or not some people liked steak.

Nita offered to drive if Ellen would rather not and she relinquished the keys gladly. She sat back feeling very secure and confident in Nita's ability to drive so fast through the vicious weather.

They got out and went quickly under the protecting canopy to the theater building. A doorman parked the car and Ellen found herself swept into a world of elegant people dressed in high fashion evening clothes. Nita took her by the elbow and Ellen felt proud to be in the company of a person who looked almost regal in this gathering of the town's upper crust.

Nita wore a white chiffon dress that defied the weather or anything else to spoil her appearance. She wore just a touch of emerald placed in a design that carried an observer's eye gracefully from the lovely white breast upward to the wide-placed eyes. Beside her Ellen felt like a child just learning the methods of beauty. She felt little and demure and all the exquisitely feminine things that give a woman confidence.

Apparently Nita was accustomed to going places without Charles. She did not display any of the helplessness which Ellen would feel if she had to attend an occasion without the benefit of a male escort.

Nita introduced her to various people who had come in from out of town. Ellen recognized the names of some of them. Celebrities in the field of science.

"Richard Wayne," Nita said, allowing the spectacled young gentleman to take her hand. "How marvelous that you could manage to get here." She turned immediately to Ellen.

"Mrs. Tendler, I'd like you to meet an old travelling friend of mine. We used to go skiing together before bio-chemistry stole him away from me."

Nita was cordial and charming and friendly and lovely. All the qualities of a perfect hostess came from her apparent natural delight. And yet Ellen felt that she was playing a part of some kind. Far more than her heart, Nita's mind seemed to control the warmth that she gave to people.

When the lights dimmed at curtain time, Ellen noticed that there was no empty seat waiting for Charles.

The performance was a drawing-room comedy and Ellen allowed herself to enjoy the amusing banter. When the lights went on again at the end of the first act, she hesitated to ask Nita about Charles. Perhaps she had given away his ticket at the last minute. No doubt the weather could have detained him. Or maybe the operation had developed unforeseen complications. There were a dozen reasonable excuses for his absence.

During the second and third acts, the growing heat in the theater began to make Ellen uncomfortable. Her throat was not sore any longer, but her head had taken on a woozy sensation that prevented her from thinking clearly. She felt very weak, almost giddy.

Occasionally Nita glanced at her in the semi-darkness but Ellen did not look back. She wanted Nita to see how much she was enjoying herself. She wanted Nita to know how very glad she was that she had been asked.

When the performance was over, Ellen stood quietly by and listened to Nita refuse half a dozen invitations for them to join after-theater parties. Ellen was glad that Nita did not want to prolong the evening. She needed to get to bed and sleep away the discomfort in her system.

Richard Wayne found them in the crowd and offered to get their wraps from the coat room.

"Yes, please," Nita said. "Mrs. Tendler isn't feeling very well and I'd hate to leave her alone in the crush."

Curiously Ellen looked from Nita's face to Dr. Wayne's. She hadn't said a word about feeling ill. And she certainly had done everything possible to hide it.

When he had gone off with the coat checks, Ellen said, "Do I look that bad?"

Nita opened her purse and took out the car keys. "No," she said. "But I didn't think you wanted to get involved with Dick."

"You like him."

"Yes, of course I like him. But trust me about Richard. He's what you call a hanger-on. One word of encouragement and he'll be with us for the rest of the night."

Ellen felt too tired to inquire further. Dr. Wayne seemed like a likeable enough sort. All the undercurrents about Nita which she had begun to notice were too much for her now.

"As a matter of fact," Ellen said, "I really don't feel well at all."

Nita turned Ellen's chin up and looked hard into her eyes. "Why didn't you say so earlier? We didn't have to come out this evening. You've probably gone and caught yourself all kinds of germs in this weather."

"I didn't want to spoil our evening."

"Oh child."

As they stood thus engrossed with each other, Richard Wayne returned carrying their coats over his arm.

"What say I drive you people home?" he offered. Behind his thick glasses, Richard's eyes seemed to see a lot more than he appeared to know. Maybe peering into a microscope had given him that intense appearance and it didn't really mean anything. Yet Ellen felt that if she wanted to find out anything about Nita, Richard Wayne would be the person who could enlighten her the most. She noticed that he didn't even mention Charles.

"That's good of you, Dick," Nita said. "But we can make it home quite all right, thank you."

"As you like," he said. Then quite unexpectedly he took Ellen's hand. "I hope you'll be feeling better very soon. And perhaps the three of us can get together before I have to leave for Paris."

"Are you going to be in town?" Nita asked. She didn't sound quite as pleased as she should have, Ellen noticed.

"Well I'm going to look in at the hospital. It has one of the finest research departments in the country, thanks to Charles."

"Then I hope you'll have time to drop by for dinner," Nita said.

Ellen knew by the tone of Nita's voice that she expected her to start moving toward the exit.

"Good bye, Dr. Wayne."

Ellen thought that he gave her a rather sad smile and then decided that it was only because of the glasses.

Nita preceded her into the car and opened the window just enough to allow a bit of the night air to cool them. The rain continued to pour in a steady flow, making the air damp and uncomfortable.

"Is that too chilly for you?" Nita asked.

"No, it's fine." Ellen was busy trying to figure out why Nita had treated her old friend in such a crisp manner. "I don't think you really do like Richard Wayne," Ellen said.

"Shall we fight about that?"

Ellen turned to see if she were serious. In profile Nita's face looked like an ancient Greek medallion. She had no expression of annoyance but neither did she have a smile. The high forehead was completely smooth and unperturbed by Ellen's accusation. She seemed to enjoy driving through the rain and her fingers were relaxed on the wheel. Ellen pulled her coat tighter around her shoulders against the chill blowing in through the slightly opened window. Riding beside Nita, bickering with her about little things, made Ellen feel somehow right. A closeness seemed to be growing between them built as much on their differences as on their agreements.

But now, as Ellen thought about it, she couldn't name one thing about which they agreed. Nor was it important. She closed her eyes and listened to the thump thumping of the wipers. Nita's smooth driving lulled her into a peacefulness which made it unimportant for her to consider what kind of relationship she was having with this woman. The ordinary elements of friendship were certainly lacking. Well, whatever it was, Ellen knew she was enjoying herself and that was all that mattered.

She felt the car stop and opened her eyes. Nita was leaning across to the back seat, reaching for the umbrella.

"You ought to come in and take a couple of pills. Charles keeps a complete supply of pharmaceuticals."

Ellen was about to object. Yet she didn't feel very much like continuing this game of matching wits. Even if she had the energy, she knew she was bound to lose. Nita had all the answers and she might as well face it now in the beginning.

She allowed Nita to hustle her into the house.

Nita took her into the living room and poured them each a glass of brandy.

"This ought to kill the germs faster than any medicine," Ellen said. "I have faith in home remedies."

Nita helped her stretch out on the couch. In her white dress she seemed like a diaphonous creature who came and went with the shadows. A soft glow of lamplight, a drink, the quiet combined to make Ellen sleepy. She smiled and allowed a yawn to escape her. Her body sank comfortably into the pillows.

"I could stay here forever," she said.

"Then perhaps you should stay for the night at least."

Something in the back of Ellen's mind warned her that she should refuse. But it was a very small voice and she didn't feel inclined to pay it any attention. There must be plenty of room for her in this large house. She had no reason to go home since Warrie would be gone for the night. It was after one o'clock. Nita would have to take her home, then drive herself back, then return the car in the morning. It seemed like a good deal more trouble than if Ellen stayed over.

"Supposing I stay until Charles gets back," Ellen said in a compromise.

"That means you will stay for the night," Nita laughed. "I don't expect him until sometime next week. He's holed in at the hospital. That's his real home, you see. This place is only second best."

Gradually Ellen was beginning to realize that Nita's relationship with her husband was not the close partnership she had assumed. Obviously Nita was accustomed to going places by herself and living very much like a divorced woman. As this idea came across to her, Ellen began to regret all the words she had spoken earlier this evening. No wonder Nita could not imagine why any woman should envy her. In her own way she must be surely alone as Ellen felt.

"I had a wonderful time tonight," Ellen said. "I'm glad you asked me."

Nita was sitting on a Queen Anne chair, her arms resting on the blue velvet. She smoked now with the ivory cigarette holder and her face behind the wisps of smoke seemed very far away.

"How are you feeling?" she said in a voice just loud enough for Ellen to hear.

"Better, thank you." She didn't really feel better at all. Yet she didn't want to trouble Nita with the petty problem of her health. She wished she were better company with sparkling conversation. All of Nita's friends must have sparkling conversation, she thought.

Ellen's limbs had once again begun to take on that sensation of unreality which she had experienced when she was powdering Nita's back. This feeling seeped slowly upward as she looked at the woman. Ellen wanted to get behind that screen of smoke. She wanted Nita to tell her important, personal details of her life. But even in her semi-wakefulness Ellen knew that this was an unreal hope. She could believe that very few people indeed knew the secret of Nita Probish's mind. Perhaps Richard Wayne understood. And perhaps that was the reason she had not wished Ellen to get to know him better.

"I think you'd better go to bed now," Nita said.

Ellen wanted to go to bed. And yet she wanted to stay awake and continue to probe the intrigue of this beautiful woman who had for some reason taken such a liking to her.

"Come on," Nita urged. "Let's get you into some pajamas."

Ellen hadn't worn pajamas since her eighteenth birthday. Without arguing, she went with Nita into the bedroom and turned so that Nita could unzip her dress. She enjoyed these ministrations almost as though she had a right to them.

"I can do the rest," she said and moved away from the touch of Nita's fingers. She wanted privacy. But how could she expect Nita to realize this when she had undressed and taken a bath in her presence?

But Nita saved her further embarrassment by leaving her on the pretext of going for another bathrobe.

As Ellen climbed into the brand new cotton pajamas, she wondered if she were supposed to sleep in Nita's bed. She certainly expected that this house had at least one guest room.

"Are you decent?" Nita said before reentering.

The question brought a violent flush to Ellen's cheeks. She blamed the confusion she felt on the fever she knew burned through her body. There was no mistaking the dry warmth consuming her. Ellen felt ill and she knew the only sensible thing would be for her to get into bed without further thought or attempt at sociability.

She looked at Nita questioningly.

"That bed is large enough for both of us, don't you think?" Nita said.

Yes, it was tremendously large. The clean high pillows beckoned her and Ellen crawled in without comment. She tried to wait while Nita put out the lights, but eyelids closed heavily long before the woman returned.

It had been many years since Ellen had slept in another's bed. Restlessly she turned in her sleep and tried to punch the pillow into a familiar shape. The mattress beneath her had a different resiliency from her own. She awoke into the darkness thirsting for a glass of water. The awareness of another person's body beside her made Ellen feel more secure than she had been for a long long time. She knew that if she really needed anything, she could touch the sleeping form and it would awaken to help her.

But she didn't want to disturb Nita. The woman slept with one arm embracing the pillow as it might a lover. In the darkness Ellen could make out the shape of the head and the pajama collar turned up to the neck. She wouldn't disturb the sleeping figure for so small a thing as a glass of water. Ellen lay very still, trying to fall asleep again. But the dryness in her throat increased until finally she moved as quietly as possible out of bed and went to the faucet in the bathroom.

All went well until she turned on the tap.

"Something wrong?" Nita's voice, heavy with sleep, came to her.

"No. I'm just getting some water."

"Sure that's all?"

"Yes. Go back to sleep."

Ellen filled the glass and took a few swallows. She realized that she must have been dreaming unspeakable dreams. Her body was too alive. That familiar tenseness pulsed through her thighs. Only her illness saved Ellen from feeling ashamed of herself. She could not worry about morals, feeling the way she did.

As she stood in the bathroom, Ellen tried to remember whether it was Raoul or Jay or her husband who had come to her in sleep and aroused the unwanted passions that irritated her now into complete wakefulness. But she could not remember. She rinsed out the glass and went back to bed. Did Nita suffer from a similar problem, she wondered. Surely if her husband were gone most of the time, she must have some difficulties of a physical nature.

But Nita seemed to be sleeping very peacefully again.

The next morning Ellen awoke with a raging fever. She could barely move her head. Her lips felt dry and cracked as though she were lying in the tropic sun. She felt beside her in the bed and discovered that it was empty.

She lay still, thinking that she had to get home before Warrie. When she tried to sit up, it took all her effort to move. The dull gray light which came in through the curtained windows made her squint. The rain had apparently stopped because all was soundless. Now and then a bird twittered as though peeking out between the leaves to see if all was clear.

Nita came in with a bed tray and set it over Ellen's legs.

"Want to try a little breakfast?" she said.

Ellen shook her head. The thought of making any movement, even to feed herself, seemed impossible.

"Well, let's see what the thermometer says." She placed it under Ellen's tongue and sat down on the edge of the bed to wait.

Nita looked like she had had a good night's sleep. Her hair was combed neatly in place and she seemed very calm. Ellen could tell this from the careful way she handled the thermometer.

"You'll do," Nita said, after reading the thermometer and shaking it down. "A hundred point three isn't too much for you to cope with," she smiled. "Get these capsules down and you'll be fine by this evening."

Ellen raised herself on one elbow and swallowed the elephant-sized capsules. She wanted to thank Nita for her kindness and apologize for making a nuisance of herself, but the moment she started Nita quieted the words.

"I know that Warren's on your mind," she said. "I can go to your place and meet him."

"No," Ellen said in a deep rough voice that sounded nothing like her own. "I'll drive back myself."

"That wouldn't be exactly wise."

Ellen waved her hand with annoyance. She wasn't going to lie here like a helpless infant.

"All right," Nita said. "I know better than to argue with you about that, little mother."

With Nita's help, Ellen managed to get herself out of bed and into a pair of Nita's slacks and a shirt. She forced herself to drink a cup of tea and eat a soft boiled egg. Then she insisted on driving herself home.

Since the rain had stopped and the roads this early on a Sunday morning were clear of traffic, Nita did not protest.

"I'll come by to see you later on," Nita said as Ellen made her way to the car.

Ellen reached her house and went right back to bed. She did not feel any more comfortable in her own place than she had at Nita's. In fact, she missed the little attentions. The lack of them only pointed up how much she couldn't bear being alone. If she wanted an aspirin, she would have to get out of bed. If she wanted some hot broth, she would have to get up and make it herself. Warrie might not be home until very late in the afternoon. They were hiking back, she remembered. For a moment, Ellen regretted leaving Nita's place so soon.

Even if Raoul were with her, it would be better than nobody. At a time like this, when she couldn't take care of herself physically, Ellen knew that she'd better keep a tight grip on her emotions. She had a way of getting angry with herself that could lead her to do fitful things that she might regret later.

She thought about phoning Raoul. He would come over. And she would feel no qualms about making him cater to her. What saved Ellen from doing this was that she didn't want him to see her looking so terrible. Whether or not she cared for the man was entirely beside the point.

But if she were thinking about him as somebody to help her, perhaps she really did care for him. Was it possible that she could feel anything but loathing for Raoul? Again, she blamed this on the fever. Her mind, distorted by illness, could hardly be expected to work normally. To save herself, Ellen let her mind play back over Warren. She lay quite still, remembering the thousand different expressions of his kindness.

As she lay thus, somewhat more at peace with herself, she heard the front door open.

Nita came in carrying Ellen's evening dress.

"How's it going?" she said, hanging the dress into the closet and taking off her raincoat.

Ellen shrugged. She hadn't expected Nita so soon but she was glad that the woman had come.

"I'm getting better, already," she said.

"Good. I'd rather not worry about you."

Worry about her? Certainly she wasn't so ill that she had to worry about her.

"You're convincing me that I'm ill," Ellen said.

"I just wanted to remind you to hurry up and get well quickly. The bus just dropped my boy off. Yours will be here any minute."

Now Ellen was truly grateful that the woman had come over. If Jay decided to stop in for a minute, Nita could make apologies for her. She wondered if it would be a good idea to explain to Nita about Jay.

"Will you do me a favor?" Ellen said.

"Of course."

"Will you keep Warrie out of this room and make my apologies to his teacher?"

Ellen noticed a hint of amusement come into Nita's eyes. She wondered how well Nita was acquainted with Jay and what she thought of him. Not that her opinion could make any difference, really.

"I'd be happy to do that," Nita said. "Jay Masters has a habit of making himself at home wherever he goes."

Then she did know him. And apparently much better than Ellen did. She wanted to hear more.

But Nita was no more willing to talk about Jay Masters than she wanted to tell her about Richard Wayne last night. She switched the conversation to Warrie and asked permission to make him some lunch if he came in hungry.

Ellen lay very still and attentive when Nita went to answer the door bell's ring.

She could make out Jay's voice and heard Warrie come clattering through the house. But she could not get the whole conversation between Nita and Jay, beyond the conventional words she had commissioned Nita to say on her behalf.

She had the distinct feeling that there was some kind of ill will between them. Yet she could not imagine anyone not liking Jay. If Nita had some special information or knowledge about him, she wanted to know what it was before allowing Warrie or herself to become too involved with the man. For an instant, she felt almost well enough to get out of bed so she could witness what was going on.

Then the door closed and she heard Nita calling Warrie back from his charge toward the bedroom. She listened to Nita explaining with tremendous tact that his mother wasn't feeling very well today. Nita understood how to curb his high spirits without subduing them. Warrie quieted almost instantly and accepted the offer of a glass of milk and a sandwich.

But before he went into the kitchen with her, he came to the door and said, "Hey, Mom, I hope you feel better soon. We sure had a good time."

His voice gave Ellen a lift. The sense of unreality faded with the sound of Warrie's voice. Perhaps she was too wound up with being a mother. But it was the largest happiness in her life. This was all the answer she needed in her mind against Nita's evaluation.

She didn't want Warrie to go out and find somebody to play with. Pulling together all her strength, Ellen got out of bed and slipped into a warm skirt and sweater. She wanted to sit down with Warrie and hear all about the day's adventure.

Bundling herself up well, she went into the kitchen and sat down opposite him.

Nita looked at her with disapproval but she didn't care. There was no time for her to be sick now. Warrie was much more important.

Nita opened a can of chicken broth and heated it for her as Ellen asked her son questions.

"We had a peachy time, all right. And you know what?" He pushed the empty glass away and licked the milk from the edges of his lips. "Mr. Masters is going to teach us how you tie all those knots they use on ships. He was a sailor."

Behind Warrie's back, Nita lifted a knowing eyebrow as she went about the business of spooning the soup into a dish.

"He told me I could stay after school tomorrow and help get the ropes together."

Warrie's enthusiasm did more for Ellen than all the capsules and brandy.

"Then it's all right with you if he comes to dinner some time during the week?"

"Sure, Mom. I never said it wasn't."

Ellen went to get herself a spoon and took the dish from Nita's hands. "I really am much better," she said.

"So I see." Nita had poured herself a plate of the soup. She sat at the other end of the table, watching Ellen and Warrie in conversation.

Finally Warrie said, "I'm going out for a walk. We didn't hike back after all. The roads were so slippery. I'll come back for supper."

After he left Ellen cleared away the dishes. "If you have anything to say about Jay Masters, I'd like to hear it."

Nita lit a cigarette and crossed her legs. She didn't seem disturbed by the question, but then again, Nita's face wasn't the kind that showed emotion readily.

"All I know about Jay Masters is that he's a good school teacher who thinks he'd make an even better father. Which is all right, I suppose, for boys who don't ..."

"Have any fathers," Ellen finished for her.

"Yes, Ellen, that's just the point."

Ellen leaned against the sink as Nita reached across the table and brought an ash tray closer.

"It's none of my business, of course," Nita said in a lower tone.

"I want to know everything I can about him," Ellen said. "To be honest with you, I think Warrie needs him."

"Well he can't do Warrie any harm." She emphasized the boy's name in such a way as to imply that perhaps Jay could do other people harm, namely Ellen herself.

"That's all that interests me, Nita. I'm looking out for the good of my son, which I'm sure you know already."

Outside the clouds had begun to disperse and growing fragments of blue threw light into the room.

"I didn't mean to alarm you." Nita crossed her legs and smiled ruefully. She seemed genuinely sorry for having caused Ellen to think wrongly of Jay Masters' intentions.

"Maybe I'd better go now," Nita said. "I don't think you're going to stay in bed any more today."

"Nita, please. I didn't mean to question you. Believe me, I value every word you say." Ellen came over and sat down beside her. Without thinking she took Nita's hands in her own and held them tightly. "I don't want you to go. Not angrily."

Nita extricated her hands with gentleness.

"We are friends," Ellen persisted. "Nobody but a friend could have treated me with the kindness you've shown."

"Yes, we are friends. But I do have a lot of things to accomplish today. We'll be seeing each other. Call me one of these days."

Though her mind worked frantically, Ellen could think of nothing to say as Nita went off for her coat and said good bye.

Supposing Nita thought her a selfish fool? Supposing she believed that Ellen had only wanted to use her for the moment. Ellen didn't know what to do in order to make it up to her. She hadn't wanted to hurt Nita's feelings. But the important point was that she had succeeded in doing that very thing.

Nita's kindness didn't deserve this shoddy reciprocation. Somehow she must show the woman how much respect and sincere liking she felt for her.

Ellen went out onto the back terrace, trying to think how to solve her latest problem.

She was not accustomed to the need for ingratiating herself with another woman. It was like having to learn to speak another language.

Warrie came home and brought Jay Masters with him.

"You said we should all have dinner together. I told Mr. Masters and he agreed."

Ellen didn't have an inch of make-up on her face, but somehow she felt that it wasn't important.

"Yes, I thought it was an excellent idea." He smiled at Ellen as though she were dressed like a princess. She had almost forgotten the fireside glow that came to Jay's face when he grinned. "But instead of you doing the cooking…"

"Oh no," Ellen protested. She couldn't go through another session of Warrie's and Jay's acrobatics with the dishes.

"Wait a minute," Jay said. "Don't be hasty. We ordered dinner to be sent up from Wo Ming. How about that?"

"Yeah," Warrie said. "How about that?"

Ellen felt a sensation of joy spread through her that erased all her worries about Nita and her preoccupation with the challenge of Raoul. *This* was living. She didn't care if everybody in the universe hated Jay Masters. She and Warrie were on his side.

"Besides," Jay added, "you're not supposed to be feeling so well."

"Oh I'm feeling just grand." Ellen's voice soared away almost beyond reach. "Just grand."

She knew with complete certainty that Jay Masters was not interested in her as Warrie's mother. No man would go out of his way so far if his interest were purely professional. After a day and night of being with children, he would want to take it easy. And he had chosen to spend the evening with her. Surely if Warrie had gone to him with the invitation to supper, he could have postponed it for another night. But no. He had wanted to be with her.

Ellen took his top coat and hung it beside her own. She stood looking at the broad shouldered coat taking up as much space as three of hers. This masculine touch was just what the closet needed for balance. Perhaps some day she could look down and see a few pairs of his shoes sitting beside her heels. Ellen decided right then and there to pursue Jay Masters with everything she could muster. Once, if only once she could get him to put his arms around her, she would become so alluring, so desirable that he would never allow her to be free for anyone else.

The three of them went into Warrie's room and looked over his album of baseball pictures. Warrie sat in the middle and Ellen noticed how long Jay's legs were when he sat beside her son. She needed the sound of his footsteps in the house.

"You know something? My mother used to be pitcher on her school softball team."

Jay looked at her with a mixture of delight and surprise. "Is that so?"

Ellen nodded. She hadn't realized that Warrie remembered her efforts to try to be a companion to him. Of course she had been a substitute pitcher, but it hadn't seemed important to tell that to Warrie. She was hardly known as a paragon of athletic prowess and Ellen was grateful that men were not attracted to women for their ability to throw a curve ball over the plate.

But she could imagine Jay coaching a group of youngsters. That element of sportsmanship which appealed to children appealed also to Ellen. She liked the thought of a healthy masculine body conquering her own. The element of sunlight in sex drew her to him. His straight forward manner had more attraction for her than all the intrigue and drinking and orgies which had been hinted to her at Raoul's party.

As Jay and Warrie spoke about methods of lighting campfires, Ellen thought of Jay coming to her after a day in the outdoors. She could almost hear him singing off key in the shower. And what would it be like to hand him a towel as he stepped out onto the bathmat? Would he grab her to him and kiss her without regard for the water getting all over her clothes? That would be delicious.

The errand boy arrived with his packages of food and while Ellen put things into plates, Warrie and Jay set the table.

Capturing Jay seemed so easy to her now. And so necessary to her well-being. She could live once again, the healthy routined life for which she craved. And if Jay could still the gnawing ache in her body, she would dedicate herself to him forever.

Ellen could find no reason for Nita to dislike him. Unless Nita had decided purposely to keep something from her.

CHAPTER FIVE

E LLEN's decision to lead Jay Masters into a serious affair gave a new purpose and direction to her usual routine. She had come into possession of a definite goal. No more futile wandering among vague dreams of happiness. And Ellen believed that she could do much for Jay in return. His teacher's salary could not buy him the luxurious comforts of living. She remembered the first day when he had admired her automobile. Jay wanted a good car and a comfortable home. He appreciated material acquisitions. If Jay would marry her, he could have both the spiritual pleasures of his career and the financial benefits of Ellen's assistance.

And, more important than all her other thoughts, Ellen thought that she could love Jay Masters. Not with the spontaneous desire which had exalted her marriage to Warren. But this second, quieter flame could shed light too.

On Monday morning, Ellen received a box of long-stemmed roses. Swiftly she pulled the card out of its small envelope and read: *I hope we can see each other next weekend. Raoul.*

Of course, she had wanted the flowers to come from Jay. But he wasn't the suave type of man to make this kind of gesture. The roses were huge American beauties and they had been wired from New York. Ellen arranged them in a milk glass vase, considering how she might go about discouraging Raoul. She didn't want to get even with him. In fact, now that she felt so certain of her desire for Jay, she could afford to be kindly disposed toward Raoul. She could easily love the whole world with a motherly affection. But Raoul would not consent to a mere friendship. He would persist until his ego, or whatever was bothering him, were satisfied.

But Ellen was in no mood to think about anything but Jay. She had much to do. He liked her cooking, he liked Warrie. Somehow, she must arouse his passion so that his liking would become an insatiable need.

The art of seduction was not part of Ellen's equipment. She had never needed guile to achieve her purposes. And she realized that Jay wasn't the kind of man who succumbed to perfume and low cut necklines. What would entice him? If just once she could get him to kiss her, the biggest obstacle would be out of the way. Perhaps if she could get him to take her on a picnic...

Indian summer had gone with the rains and a nippy air replaced the last touches of warm weather. A hike in the hills would be delightful and the exercise would do her a lot of good. Ellen decided to phone Jay and invite him to go with her.

Not only did Jay accept, but he suggested that they take Warrie along. This was more than Ellen had hoped for. If Warrie and Jay became close friends, her son could not resent a second marriage.

They planned to go Wednesday after school. Ellen went to town and purchased frankfurters and marshmallows. She knew a site where they could build a bonfire. After she bought the food, Ellen made a special purchase and a more personal one. She had to be feminine to lure Jay, but feminine in a sporty way. She bought a red jacket with a high knit collar which would bundle up around her ears and make her look very different from the men in their plain lumber jackets. She saw a pair of western trousers and decided to try them on. The legs were cut very narrow and the black material emphasized the well-shaped legs. She felt satisfied that this costume would appeal to Jay, just as her evening clothes would appeal to a more conventional man. A pair of black mittens to match completed the costume.

Ellen returned home thinking how really fortunate she was. Because of Raoul she had come very close to getting involved level. But the more she tried the more her efforts were rewarded with vivid imaginings about making love.

Ellen went about her household chores, spurred on by the restless expectancy of Jay's hands caressing her in the dark private shadows of night. She thought of her head lying on his chest and inhaling the vibrant outdoor odor of his skin. The controls she usually tried to place upon her mind had all left her. Nothing could soothe or change the direction of her thought until her body had united in a satisfying act of love.

Wednesday finally arrived and Ellen put on her new outfit. She looked very young and almost like a pixie. The bulky jacket concealed the heaving of her breasts and she snuggled inside it with the pleasure of expecting Jay's fingers to probe beneath the material.

When Warrie and Jay arrived, she was waiting at the door for them. She had packed the food in a wicker basket and it sat on the doorstep beside her.

"Hey Mom," Warrie called. "You look like one of the girls in my class."

She glanced at Jay and saw the approval in his eyes. "Warren's right," he said. "But with a difference."

"What kind of difference?" Warrie put in. "She isn't so tall either."

"Will one of you men take the basket?" Ellen said.

Warrie looked at the basket and sighed. "Couldn't you put it into a ruck sack?"

"It'll be all right like this," Jay said, quieting Warrie's objection.

The three of them started off down the road with Ellen walking in the middle. Already she felt as though they composed a family. She strode along, keeping up with their brisk pace and lifting her chin to the wind. With each deep breath she felt stronger and gayer. Her world was bright. Almost complete. What could be better than to spend an afternoon in the country with her men, then come home and fulfill the impulses brought on by cold air and physical exercise?

As they climbed into the hills, Ellen promised herself that she would not let Jay go home tonight before kissing her. They went deeper into the woodland, disturbing rabbits out of their statuesque positions. Warrie ran ahead of them, climbing over boulders and in general making the path more difficult for himself. His eyes were wide open with a healthy appetite for life. So different from the sullen child she had known less than a week ago. She must let Jay know how very grateful she was to him for this.

They reached the charred spot where many campers had built their campfires. Jay set down the basket and Warrie went off to collect dry twigs. Ellen pulled off her mittens and sat down cross-legged on the grass as Jay made a neater circle of the rocks for the fireplace.

"This was one of your best ideas," he said. The wind tossed his hair into circlets of gold and his cheeks were almost apple red. He looked hardly more than a boy himself and Ellen felt that together the three of them could stay young like this forever.

"You're teaching me how to live," she said to Jay. "I'm having the best time of my life." The words were sincere and Ellen didn't feel embarrassed to express them. She felt that maybe Jay needed a little encouragement.

"Good," Jay said. "That's what I'm here for." He stood up and dusted off his hands. "I think I'll bring all the kids here this weekend. It's a fine spot."

Ellen understood that Jay had a right to be concerned with his professional duties. But she wished he would stop thinking about them for the time being. She had never known a teacher to take his job this seriously. For most it was nine to three, then forget about it until the next day. Truly Jay was an inspired person in his field. But he needn't overdo it.

"There are lots of places I can show you," Ellen said, thinking of Frog Pond. She wondered if it might be better, the first time, to have him make love to her in the open. He preferred the outdoors. Jay's bigness blended in with the spread of nature. She could imagine his room with all the windows wide open at night.

"You've lived here all your life, Ellen. I'd be glad if you could show me around. I still feel like a tourist." He was glancing past her as he spoke. "I hope Warren doesn't think he has to collect a whole forest. Must remember to tell the boys about the principles of making a fire."

Ellen sighed and leaned back on her palms. How on earth could she get him to concentrate on her for awhile?

"Jay, I have something to confess to you."

"About Warrie?"

Yes, it was about Warrie, but she wished he hadn't said it so quickly and attentively.

Ellen nodded. "I can't get him to do the assignments."

"A little patience. He'll come along." Jay went to the basket and Ellen came over also.

"I'll do that," she said. "A woman's privilege."

She lifted the lid and took out a package of cellophane wrapped frankfurters. Next time they went out, even if it was for another hike, she was going to make certain that it would be just the two of them. Alone.

Warrie returned and Ellen sat back as Jay showed him how to construct a pyramid of paper, twigs and wood so that a fire would kindle and burn evenly. As she thought back into the past, Ellen realized that Warrie hadn't shared this much rapport with his own father. Of course the boy had been so much younger. That could be the reason. And yet, Jay had such an instinctive way with children. Their conversations seemed to hold Ellen at a distance. She wasn't quite sure that this pleased her as much as she had thought it would.

But there was still tonight. Comforted with the thought that Warrie had to go to bed by nine, Ellen let them enjoy themselves and only participated when she felt it was natural to do so.

After they had eaten, Jay killed the fire and they started toward home. Walking downhill required less effort. Jay lit his pipe and smoked in long puffs snatched brusquely by the wind.

The sun had dipped over the last hill by the time they reached Ellen's house. She took Jay inside and extended her hand for his jacket before he could say anything about having to go back to his own place. But Ellen realized she had no reason to fear this, because he didn't seem in the least bit impatient to leave. Jay settled himself in the living room and Warrie came to him with his homework.

At seven o'clock they all watched a television program and Ellen saw Warrie stifling yawn after yawn. Usually getting him to bed was a problem. But all this activity conspired against him. By eight thirty Warrie excused himself and went off to bed.

Ellen did not bother to change out of the tight trousers. They did as much for her figure as a dress. This costume, so difficult for most women to wear well, complimented her lithe frame. She wore a tight fitting sweater tucked into the pants and in it her breasts stood outward and upward. The tissue thin wool showed no excess flesh beneath the band of her brassiere.

Jay opened the collar of his sport shirt and accepted an offer for coffee. Ellen brought in the cups and stirred the right amount of sugar and cream into his.

"You know me pretty well," Jay laughed.

She liked the shadow of beard which had begun to darken his cheeks. Ellen wanted to rub her own face against it and enjoy the roughness.

"I'd like to know you a great deal better," she said. The tips of her fingers and toes were still warm and tingling from the afternoon's hike. But she could not distinguish this from the other more animal warmth that flooded her. The two blended into a teeming of desire and she sat down on the couch close enough for him to take her in his arms if he wanted to.

"There isn't much to know about me," Jay said. He jammed his hands into his trousers pockets and stretched out his legs. "I'm just a plain hick school teacher."

"But a man can't live on that alone," Ellen ventured. She didn't know how far she could go without Jay realizing that she was the aggressor. That was the worst thing to do to a man, she knew. But one of them had to make a move. She didn't have the patience to wait until Jay finally got around to it. Supposing he had the benefit of a mistress? If he were satisfied that way, he could afford to dally with her as long as it pleased him.

"Maybe it sounds like a joke," Jay said, "but I'm very satisfied with what I'm doing. You know, some men have dreams of running a business or owning real estate all over the country. I don't aspire to anything that grandiose. I don't think life's big enough for a man to do many things to the best of his ability. If I can motivate a couple of kids to go on and accomplish their own dreams, then I'm satisfied."

"And you'd have a right to be," Ellen said. She wished he would look directly at her when he talked instead of staring off at the carpet as though she weren't in the room with him.

"Coming from you, that's a compliment," Jay said. "I can see that you're accustomed to bigger things than that."

So that was why he was hesitating. Jay must think she was looking for a man with lots of money. How foolish of her not to realize his concern sooner.

"Oh yes," Ellen said with more life than she had been feeling earlier. "My husband was a financial wizard. But that wasn't why I married him. I think that a man who is happy in his profession is the richest, most eligible bachelor."

Now Jay turned and looked at her. His face was completely serious, which made a rugged impression on Ellen. The usual softening warmth had disappeared. She wanted to grab that face and kiss it brutally.

"Since I'm happy in my profession, as you put it, does that make me the most eligible bachelor?"

Ellen nodded. She heard Jay clear his throat. Had she made him uncomfortable? Did he feel that she was forcing something which should develop slowly and naturally between two people? They hadn't known each other very long. Supposing Ellen's desire showed through here facade of casual interest.

"I'm very fond of you, Ellen. You're the only woman in town who has really made me feel at home, except my landlady."

"It hasn't been all for Warrie's sake, you know. Although that did play a large part in my interest. At first."

Jay took out his pipe again and clamped it between his teeth. He couldn't kiss her if he were smoking a pipe, she thought irritably.

"That's good," he said around the stem. "That's really good."

"Are you sure?"

She looked at him straight forwardly. It seemed accidental that her breast was pressing against his arm. The night wind had begun to howl outside, whipping the last leaves from the limbs of the trees.

"You know," Ellen said, "sometimes a woman isn't quite sure how a man will interpret her hospitality. Especially a woman who has a child and enough money so she doesn't have to work. I wouldn't blame a man for thinking that such a woman was only playing with him." Ellen felt that the words were hardly smooth. They didn't sound calculated. They were scarcely the polished, guileful things that other women used to attain their ends. But Ellen had at her command nothing more than her desire to let Jay know how much she admired and needed him as a lover and husband.

"I understand about you, Ellen," he said. "Please don't think that you must tell me your motives are honest. I know they are."

Still he didn't make a move to touch her. Ellen could hardly stand this closeness without any hint of consummation. She had to get through his wall of reserve. Perhaps working with children had made him accustomed to considering all things except the sexual impulse.

"We'll have many wonderful times together," Jay said. "I was looking forward to a lonely winter but now I know it will be different."

"Yes, it will be different for us both," Ellen murmured. She reached across and took Jay's hand. "You'll come often to supper, won't you?"

She felt his first response in the pressure of his fingers.

"I'll be here as often as you invite me."

"Tomorrow night?"

"With pleasure."

They sat for awhile in silence. Ellen could think of nothing more to say without betraying her anxiety. He was used to dealing with children and she could understand his tendency to spill this over into his other relationships. She would have to knock down his barriers evening by evening until he finally realized the physical manhood within him.

Ellen wasn't so sure she could wait too much longer. The episode with Raoul had dislodged whatever barriers she had left. Her desire screamed to be acknowledged and sated. But she must not descend upon Jay too quickly.

Because of school next morning, he left early. He still had some lesson assignments to prepare. Ellen didn't try to coax him to stay on. No matter how long he remained with her, she knew that he wouldn't move to take her in his arms.

But Ellen felt satisfied that the first step toward Jay had been accomplished. Tomorrow, she would make another small movement in his direction. Night after night she would work on him until he weakened beneath the intensity of her desire.

She took a long hot shower in an effort to soak out the aching in her muscles. There was no relaxing in Jay's presence. If she had let go for one instant, she could not trust herself not to do something that would put her to shame. With other men, a kiss was just a casual expression. With Jay it might mean the difference between having him and alienating him altogether. Ellen could not yet judge how far she could go with him.

The next morning another bouquet of American beauties was delivered to her. Ellen glanced at the card, then tossed it into the waste paper basket. Raoul was making a nuisance of himself. But how was he to know that Ellen had other interests? If Jay hadn't come into her life, she might be tempted to continue playing along with Raoul. But she wanted no part of it now. She wished for nothing to mar her conscience.

As Ellen considered her conscience, she remembered Nita and what had happened between them. She wondered what Nita must be thinking of her and what Nita would begin to think if she knew what was happening between Jay and herself. The more she thought about Nita, the more she wondered why Nita didn't want her to get to know Richard Wayne. Perhaps Nita was soured on men altogether. If her marriage had fallen apart, she might not trust people like Jay who, as Nita said, walked in and made themselves at home.

But Ellen didn't want to get in touch with Nita now. They might wind up having another argument and Ellen didn't feel up to this. She wanted Nita to approve of everything she did. And Nita would certainly detect and disapprove of her growing relationship with Jay. Ellen did not honestly know what she should do about Nita. Conscience told her to get in touch with the woman. Yet she could not bring herself to lift the receiver for fear of another impasse.

Ellen did not realize that the decision to see or not see certain people lay beyond her personal control. Though she might attempt to guide the direction of her social life, she hadn't the kind of authoritative manner to shut herself away from those who wanted to continue a friendship which she began. Because she had spent three years without anyone, Ellen believed that she had the power to discriminate when actually, she had only the primitive ability to go from one extreme to another.

Concerning Nita, she thought it best to write the woman a note. If Nita took kindly to Ellen's overture, they might be able to smooth over their differences and pursue a less intense relationship than the one already started. Ellen wanted Nita. She could learn much from the woman. But she did not want Nita to be the guiding hand in her private affairs. Ellen did not enjoy feeling like a child in awe of some mysterious goddess. But she would sincerely regret having to relinquish Nita's friendship completely.

With much thought, she composed a short letter to Nita inviting her to dinner with Charles, if she wished. It did not seem right to Ellen that Nita should have a social life completely divorced from her husband. She remembered how, at the theater, Nita's friends had automatically excluded him from the conversation. Ellen felt an instinctive sympathy toward this man. He worked hard. He supported his household well. No doubt, Charles had his shortcomings. But if Nita chose to continue her marriage, Charles should not be neglected so completely. Vaguely Ellen wished that she could spend an evening with Richard Wayne and learn something more about this woman who could be so generous and yet so difficult.

Ellen promptly put these thoughts away after she mailed the letter. Jay would be arriving soon for dinner. She had to dress and set the table. As she placed the silver, Ellen wondered if Jay would notice the roses. The deep red petals imposed a lush beauty and exuded a heavy fragrance which might attract his attention. Of course Ellen could say that she bought them herself. But Jay might not ask her. Probably he would simply take for granted that she had bought them. Then it occured to Ellen that it might not be a bad idea if Jay knew she had another admirer. A twinge of jealousy could stir him to action quicker. Jay assumed that he was the only man in her life. Ellen had practically told him as much. This wasn't a compliment. No man wanted a woman who did not attract a host of other men. The element of battle was missing from her relationship with Jay. Anyone in his place would act just as complacent with her.

But there were cons to this argument as well as pros. Ellen had to beware about making Jay feel any more sensitive about the difference in their financial status. A suitor who could wire two dozen American beauties could hardly be poor.

When Jay came for dinner, Ellen saw that he had gotten his hair cropped very short.

"I like it," she said. "Makes you look like a football player." This was the kind of compliment she knew Jay would appreciate.

He ran his palm self-consciously across his temple. Apparently Ellen's remark had been unexpected. Jay didn't think very much about his appearance. The casual clothes he wore were chosen for comfort and convenience. The fact that he looked well in them could easily be an accident.

"It's better this way for the swimming class I'm starting next week."

Ellen knew that there already was an organized swimming class.

"This is a special thing," Jay continued. "Just a small group for the disabled kids who don't want to join in with the rest."

Ellen was glad that Jay had such a generous turn. And yet it was beginning to annoy her. She didn't resent him spending time with youngsters who needed him. But she was beginning to wonder if there were a limit to Jay's sense of obligation.

Since he felt such a desire to help people, why didn't some of it come out in his relationship with Ellen? Not once had he paid her a compliment on her appearance. Jay could hardly be so stupid as not to realize that a woman thrived on such small details.

She had bothered to dress herself becomingly for him. The green jersey complimented her neat figure and the rose tones of her skin. Would it be so terrible for him to say one word to her so that she would know he appreciated her efforts for him?

"Where's Warrie?" Jay said.

"He decided to go out with the boys," Ellen responded. "I guess he's getting tired of hanging around the old folks."

To her surprise, Jay took the hint.

"I guess I'm getting tired of hanging around the young folks," he said.

Ellen nodded to herself with satisfaction. Jay's good nature could make her grim if he didn't break it up with a smattering of adult nastiness.

"Just you and me for dinner. How's that?" Ellen watched to see if he noticed the roses.

"That's the way it should be. And let's have a drink to celebrate."

Well, wasn't this an improvement. Jay's case wasn't hopeless after all. She pulled open the doors of the bar cabinet.

"Scotch? Bourbon? What'll it be, sir?" Ellen could feel the sparkle in her eyes. Her sense of being attractive returned with full assurance.

"Oh, a little bourbon'll be fine. I'll get the ice cubes."

She let Jay make himself at home in the kitchen. Maybe if he got used to lounging around, he would decide that it was a good place to be. He seemed to be in an extraordinary mood this evening. An aura of devilishness came from him. She wondered if Jay were going to commit himself to her in some way. A word. A small gift. It was too much to hope for.

He returned with the cubes and dropped some into their glasses. "I have such a good time being with you," he said and gave her an impulsive hug around the waist.

Ellen was overwhelmed. She couldn't imagine what had caused so sudden a transformation. Had he gone home the other night and thought over their words? She remained silent, waiting to hear what he would come out with next. And she remained silent because the contact of his arm with her body disturbed her more than she wanted him to see. She had to concentrate on not allowing her hand to tremble. The ice cubes would clink against the glass and give her emotions away. But she didn't want him to stop touching her. She lowered the glass to the table and turned within the circle of his arm. With a light smile as though she weren't thinking about her actions, Ellen leaned her body against Jay's. Her breasts rubbed against the tweed of his jacket. She could feel the sensation beneath the material of her dress and brassiere. Her nipples hardened and sent a little shiver through her.

"We always have a good time together," she said very softly. "And there are better times to come."

She tilted her face upward toward him and her lips parted. His arm tightened about her waist and she allowed herself to yield to the pressure. Ellen lifted her hand and stroked her palm across his ear. "I like you, Jay Masters. I like you very much."

Ellen saw his head begin to lower toward her own. Her fingers stretched out across the nape of his neck and drew him into a hard kiss. The flame in her body burst into a shower of sparks. Ellen rose on tip-toe and thrust herself against him. She could feel the ridges of his muscles even beneath the heavy jacket. Her other arm went around him and they kissed quickly many times.

"You're good for me," he muttered. "I need you."

She hoped he would carry her to the couch and prove that need. But instead, he pushed her suddenly from him.

"We'd better not get carried away with ourselves," he smiled.

She watched him straighten his jacket and sit down at the table prepared for dinner.

"Yes, it's wrong to get carried away, isn't it?" Ellen probed. She managed to keep her voice steady.

"No, it's not wrong," Jay said. "I've just been bred to be wary of hastiness. We're not adolescents at a drive-in. In all fairness to you, Ellen, I think we should wait."

"Wait for what?" Ellen said before she could stop herself. The only fair thing she could imagine would be for them to take each other. If he wanted to relax and think intellectually about their relationship, wouldn't it be wiser to placate first this irritation impulse of sex?

"Just wait, Ellen. To see how time mellows us."

She didn't want to be mellowed. Time could only destroy her. She needed him. She needed him now. How many nights could she go on without calming the force that drove her?

"Jay, if you think I'll interfere with your schoolwork, please say so now." She picked up her glass and finished its contents. The wise move would be to get dinner and finish this nonsensical talk when he had a full belly. But she couldn't be that tactful. Their desires were out in the open now. She had to follow through on her advantage or take the risk of losing the chance.

He picked up a knife and twirled it on the cloth. His silent consideration reminded her of Warrie. A simple yes or no would suffice. What was so catastrophic about two adults going to bed with each other? Surely he wasn't a virgin.

"Ellen, do you realize we haven't known each other a full two weeks?"

"One week would be more precise," she said acidly.

"One week. Can two people meet and fall in love in one week?"

"It's been done before."

He dropped the knife and put his elbows on the table, staring sightlessly past her at the roses. "I'm trying to live by the rules. For your sake more than mine."

Why did men always have to talk about love instead of doing something about it? First Raoul with his ideas about privacy. Now Jay with his consideration for her moral status. She didn't want philosophy. Her body cried out for a man to take her without conscious preliminaries. She had done enough thinking these past three years. She needed love. And she needed it right away.

"All right, darling, we'll live by the rules," she said. "What are they?"

Jay looked at her, his eyes large with puzzlement. "Oh, something about people seeing each other steadily for awhile, then getting engaged and married."

"Are you afraid I won't marry you?" she said, unconsciously twisting his meaning.

She came around to where he was sitting and put her lips down to his neck. "How long do you think it takes a woman to fall in love?"

Ellen heard him draw a long breath. "You know I'm not earning six thousand a year. I probably won't ever reach more than eight."

"Oh, that doesn't matter. You know I don't care." She came around beside him, knelt and put her cheek on his knee. "If you'd like, I'll put all my money in trust for Warrie. You'll see how happily we can live on what you earn."

Ellen realized that she was in the same position that Nita has assumed that day in her bedroom. The recollection came to her with a shock. Ellen stood up quickly, confused by the incongruous thought.

She saw that her words did not make Jay happy. He was positive about the need for more time between them. Ellen felt her advantage beginning to slip.

"I'm sorry," she said, "for being so hasty. But a woman doesn't think with the same foresight as a man. When the heart speaks, there isn't anything more to say."

Ellen left him to consider this and went into the kitchen to get dinner. A heavy disappointment weighed on her. She did not want Jay to figure out every movement of their courtship. Rules belonged in schoolbooks. He could not make love to her one lesson at a time.

The roast oozed juice. She would watch him enjoy a large helping. Mechanically she put the meat into an oval dish and brought it in for Jay's pleasure.

As he ate, Ellen poured herself more bourbon. They could go on forever without anything definite happening. She couldn't bear the thought of waiting for Jay to decide the right moment had arrived for them to take the next step in their courtship. If courtship it was. Maybe Jay was putting things off because he didn't want Ellen to trap him into something so permanent as marriage. A man of thirty was still a young bachelor. A woman of thirty, especially one who was widowed, had very little time left to find an eligible husband.

Ellen glanced up at the roses, glad that someone still thought her worth the effort.

Jay finished his dinner and helped carry the dishes back into the kitchen as was his habit.

"I hope I haven't upset you," he said.

"No," Ellen lied. "I'm glad you were intelligent enough to curb our foolish impulses."

She wished he would leave now. Ellen could think of nothing charming to talk about. Certainly she didn't want to hear him talk about the kiddies any more.

"You do understand," Jay persisted.

Oh, she understood well enough. He didn't want her. She had flung herself at him and he didn't feel inclined to catch. At least she was grateful to discover this so early in their relationship.

"Shall we go to the movies tomorrow?"

Tomorrow was Friday. No, she wouldn't go out with him. Why should he continue to think that she would wait for him?

"I'm sorry, Jay. Tomorrow night I have another appointment. An old friend from New York, you know."

"No, I don't know."

She watched him narrowly to discover if he really cared about this unnamed friend.

"Have I ever met this … person?"

He was concerned. Good. She would make him so jealous that Jay would trail her around town to see what she was doing.

"Raoul? I don't think you know Raoul. He's a prominent lawyer in New York. Those are his roses in the living room. Beautiful, aren't they?"

"Yes. Lovely. How about Saturday night, Ellen? You won't be busy with Raoul Saturday night too?"

"If you ask me not to be, I won't." She had the courage to put a little flippancy into her voice. Jay wasn't lost to her yet.

"Then Saturday night it is." He leaned over to kiss Ellen good night.

"No, Jay," she ducked her lips away from his. "Let's not rush things."

He found his jacket and Ellen saw him to the door.

CHAPTER SIX

THE EVENING had ended much earlier than Ellen had planned. But she was glad to be alone. Jay was just like every other man. Self confident and possessive. For all his outdoor manners, he still wanted a woman to tease him into action. All right, she would do just that.

But it meant going out with Raoul and maybe other men if she could find them. She didn't want to see Raoul. He knew too much about people. Of course he knew that Ellen wouldn't be able to resist his embraces. She was an easy victim for Raoul's game. Yet she had no choice now. Where would Raoul take her tomorrow night? How did he intend to torture her? She would find out soon enough.

Unconsciously Ellen filled her glass again. She was drinking double bourbons. But all she knew was that a caged monster lived inside her. A monster who was beating her into submission. She fell down onto the sofa, giddy and miserable at the same time. How could it be that the men she knew didn't want to go to bed with her? The game between male and female wasn't supposed to work this way. She must be doing something wrong. Perhaps her over-anxiety was frightening the men away.

There was nothing left but to try to go to sleep. Somehow she must escape from the labyrinth of her thoughts. She looked at her watch and saw that it was ten o'clock. It was early for her but the hour was overly late for Warrie. Her muddled brain suggested that he might be with Joey Probish. Without thinking of her decision about Nita, Ellen went to the phone and dialled her number.

No, he wasn't at their place. Nita hadn't seen him all day. Was something wrong? Ellen's voice didn't sound like herself. Was she sure there wasn't anything wrong? If Ellen wanted, she could come over right away and help her look for Warrie. Of course it wasn't necessary, but she wanted to help if she could.

Ellen thanked her and hung up. By the thank you she had really meant that Nita shouldn't bother. But within fifteen minutes she heard a car pull up in front of the house.

"You must have had a bad evening." Nita said, looking at the glass in Ellen's hand.

Ellen put the glass unsteadily on the small table in the hallway. "Not too bad," she said.

"Well, why don't you just relax and I'll scout around town a bit. He can't be too far away."

Ellen agreed. She was in no condition to go herself. And she didn't want Warrie to see her bleary eyes and mussed hair. Inside her Ellen felt very sloppy, but she took for granted that her external appearance was to blame.

Nita didn't bother to come inside. Instead she turned around and went back to her car. Ellen watched her drive away, wondering how Nita could treat her so kindly after their last meeting. Dimly Ellen told herself that Nita's faults weren't half so bad as other people's.

She put the bottle of whiskey away and washed out her glass. She couldn't go to sleep and she hated staying awake. In the whole house Ellen couldn't find a place for herself. The discomfort of her sexual cravings amounted now to an actual physical pain. Someone had to help her. Anyone.

Within the hour, Nita returned with Warrie.

"I was only doing some homework with the gang." Warrie complained. "I didn't think you'd object to that." They stood in the foyer challenging each other.

"It's true," Nita said.

"I was worried about you. You should have phoned to tell me."

Warrie sighed. "If I do something bad you don't like it. If I do something good you don't like it. You're just plain sour."

"Maybe I am," Ellen said. "Did you finish your homework?"

"How could I?"

"You can finish it now."

"I don't want to anymore."

"Then go to bed."

Nita stood with arms folded, refraining from entering into their conversation. Nevertheless Ellen could sense her disapproval. She wondered if Joey were a paragon of virtue.

Warrie stamped out of the room and both women heard him slam the door.

"Don't say a word to me, Nita. I know I'm doing it all wrong."

"You're very charming when you're tight. How about a Bromo Seltzer?"

Ellen put her hands up to stop Nita from any action. "No. I like it this way. But as long as I am tight, you listen and let me talk." Ellen felt very sure of herself. She didn't feel in awe of Nita. She felt very tall and all-knowing.

"All right. Do you mind if I sit down?"

"Good, we'll go into the living room. Where the roses are." She took Nita by the wrist and led her into the room. "Aren't they beautiful roses?"

"Yes, Ellen. Now what did you want to say to me?" She sat down in the wing chair and crossed her legs with characteristic nonchalance. She wore a tan skirt with a brown weskit that displayed the V shape of her ribline.

"First of all," Ellen said, leaning against the table. "I want you to tell me everything you know about Mr. Jay Masters."

"Oh, I see." Nita smiled that undisturbed smile which disturbed Ellen very much. "But I told you everything."

"No you didn't." Ellen felt positive and she wasn't going to let Nita get out of it now.

"I don't know how to prove it to you. I met Jay Masters early this year and he came to visit a few times. He wouldn't go away, that's all."

"Did he try to make love to you?"

"Really, Ellen. Don't get carried away with this." Nita got up, found the liquor cabinet and poured herself a drink. "May I?"

"Help yourself."

Ellen watched the fuzzy outline of Nita pick up a glass and tilt the bottle to it again. She knew in one corner of her mind that she was making a fool of herself. But the rest of her mind didn't care.

"Then he did make love to you. Otherwise you don't have enough reason to dislike him so much."

"I dislike most men, Ellen. Haven't you figured that out by now?"

Nita's words rang true. She talked about men as though they were bugs to be squashed against the wall. Ellen felt satisfied. If Nita had nothing personal against Jay, then she didn't owe Nita an apology for her warning.

"You know something?" Ellen said. "It's a good idea to be a man hater. They stink."

Nita burst out into a laugh which jarred Ellen into a semblance of alertness. She sat Ellen very carefully onto the sofa and patted her lightly on the shoulder. "You're too young to be so bitter," she said. "Wait a few years. And if you have a chance, get out on the town for awhile. The change will do you good. Different faces. You might find one that appeals to you."

"They all appeal to me," Ellen felt herself drawing close to obscenity. She didn't want to say anything off color to Nita. She might not have much left but she counted on her remaining shreds of integrity to get through her present muddle. "The trouble is," Ellen continued, "I don't appeal to anyone."

"Oh don't believe that," Nita said. "I know at least one person you appeal to." She was sitting at the other end of the couch and the light fell directly across her nose, drawing an elongated silhouette on her cheek.

"Who?" If Ellen knew one man she honestly appealed to, she would go to him immediately.

"Me," Nita said quietly. She put down her glass and folded her hands in her lap.

Ellen's mind clogged. She was certain that Nita didn't mean what she thought she had heard.

"I like you too," Ellen said. But it wasn't any comfort at all that Nita liked her. Friendship was one thing. Sex quite another. And Ellen was at the point where nothing could substitute for it.

"Oh, go to sleep," Nita said. "Tomorrow everything will look much rosier. Like the flowers."

Ellen didn't want to go to sleep. She wanted to sit up all night and talk about men. She wanted to purge her body of them. Nita would be patient. She was drunk and Nita would be very kind to her.

"Will you be good to me and not go away?" Ellen said.

"I'll be good to you and put you to bed. It isn't the same thing, of course. When you wake up, I'll be gone. But I won't leave you until you have fallen asleep."

"Then I'll stay up all night."

"We'll see."

Nita came over and forced Ellen to stand up. Despite herself, Ellen enjoyed Nita's attention. A warm, soft human being who didn't hold Ellen at a distance. She needed someone desperately. She needed arms to go around her and pull her close. She needed a human being to share one night with her.

"Let's go," Nita said.

Ellen was positive she wouldn't fall asleep. Nita would have to stay with her all night. She had promised. Ellen linked her arm through Nita's and they started off for the bedroom.

As they came through the doorway Nita switched on the lights and steered Ellen to the bed.

"Undress me," Ellen commanded. She wanted to be a child again. A child is entitled to attention. She fell back on the bed and smiled impishly at Nita. "Undress me."

She extended one foot and Nita pulled off the shoe. Then she gave her the other foot. It felt good to have someone doing things for her again. She remembered that Warren used to undress her sometimes.

"You'll have to sit up now," Nita said.

Obediently Ellen sat up. She bent her head over and felt Nita's cool fingers unhook the string of pearls. The elusive odor of jasmine came to her from Nita's closeness. Ellen leaned her cheek against the woman's shirt and inhaled deeper. It was a comfortable scent that made Ellen want to be in a hammock.

"If you'll stand up, we'll get your dress off."

Ellen was certainly enjoying herself. She wished the process would last forever. She pushed herself off the bed and raised her arms.

"That's a good girl," Nita said.

The sober compartment in Ellen's mind prayed that she wouldn't remember this foolishness in the morning. But for the moment, why shouldn't she give herself to this harmless pleasure? Everything had been going so wrong that Ellen was thankful for this little bit of catering. And Nita didn't seem to mind.

She wiggled out of her slip and turned around so Nita could unhook her bra. "I feel much better now," Ellen said as her breasts escaped from their confines. "Do you think I have a nice body?" she said. "Wouldn't men go for it?"

"I certainly think they should. Now where are your bed clothes?" Her voice had taken on a strangely stiff intonation.

"What did I do wrong now?" Ellen asked. She didn't want Nita to be angry with her. She had had enough rejection for one day.

"Did I say you've done something wrong?"

"You sound that way."

"Pajamas or a night gown?"

"But you sound angry."

Nita took a step away from the appeal in Ellen's voice. "You misunderstood, that's all."

Ellen lifted her hands and pressed the heels of her palms to her eyes. "I'm dizzy and you're angry with me." Dressed only in her panties, she sat down on the edge of the bed. See, even Nita didn't care for her.

"My night gown is in the third drawer," she said with her eyes still closed.

She heard the drawer open.

"Well, isn't this a protective covering." Nita had the happy tone in her voice again.

Ellen opened her eyes and saw Nita holding up the transparent gown. Nita looked very tall from Ellen point of view. Not only tall, but strong and very sure of herself. If Nita would stay with her, everything would turn out all right.

Ellen waited as the woman came over and slipped the nightdress over her head.

"Now under the covers and we'll tuck you in." Ellen watched as Nita pulled a chair up to the bed. She was going to sit there until Ellen fell asleep. It wasn't fair to keep her awake.

Ellen got under the covers and lay very still while Nita pulled them up to her chin. "You don't really have to stay," she said hesitantly. "But I'd like it if you would. Maybe you can spend the night here. After all, I stayed with you. It must be very late now anyhow." She wanted to have a human being with her tonight. The thought of an empty bed with cold stretches of sheet instead of bodily warmth of a person seemed almost forbidding to Ellen.

"Will you call Charles and say you're staying here?"

Nita hesitated. "I don't think it would be a good idea, Ellen."

"It's a splendid idea," Ellen felt confident. "I need something alive, Nita. There are too many ghosts with me. I don't think I can cope with them tonight."

"Yes, Ellen, I believe you." But she didn't have to make a phone call. Charles wasn't at home anyway. And Joey would sleep through the night without knowing the difference.

Nita undressed quickly and switched out the light. She didn't want a night gown. She laughed at the idea as though it were preposterous. Ellen stayed wide awake until Nita had slipped between the covers. She felt the mattress dip with the weight of this other person beside her.

Unconsciously, as Ellen drifted into sleep, she snuggled close into Nita's arms.

CHAPTER SEVEN

NITA had dressed and gone so that Ellen could not inquire how much of a fool she had acted. She very seldom got so drunk. Nor did she often need to seek oblivion so desperately. But Ellen didn't have a headache or other signs of a hangover. Mostly she regretted the letter which Nita would pick up in the mail today. It's formal tone was hardly justified after the childishness Ellen had displayed. She didn't have a right to judge anyone's way of life when her own was such a mess.

Ellen phoned Nita and told her to tear up the letter without reading it, but she called too late.

Ellen did not try to explain or apologize. The regret was so large in her heart that she could only fall silent and trust that Nita understood this through some mystical form of telepathy.

Instead of thinking about how she could handle the situation with Raoul that night, Ellen spent the day considering how best to mend things with Nita. She would do anything to prove her respect for the woman.

But, though her concerns were far from Raoul, inevitably he rang the door bell at seven o'clock.

Ellen hadn't bothered to dress for him. She didn't much want to go out anywhere. More drinking wouldn't help. They could go dancing at the country club, but she didn't care to dance. Raoul had nothing to offer Ellen that she wanted.

If Raoul noticed her lack of interest, he managed to cover it very well. He lay his topcoat over the arm of a chair and stood admiring Ellen as though they were young lovers.

"This was a long week," he said. The bankers gray suit that he wore was obviously new and well tailored to his compact body. From the sharkskin tipped shoes to the smoothly groomed hair, Raoul looked especially turned out just for Ellen. He shined with cleanliness and exuberance.

"It's been a frightful week," Ellen said. "I don't know if I'll be fit company."

"Now, now." He came over and kissed her on the cheek. "Pull yourself together and let's get out of this dismal house. You look bored to distraction."

She wasn't at all bored, except with Raoul.

"Whatever's on your mind," he said, "a change will do you good."

Oh well, as long as she did have to spend the evening with him, she might as well do her best to make the evening go along pleasantly.

"If you'll wait, I'll be dressed in a few minutes."

She went to the bedroom and took out one of her new dresses. They would be seen together and there was no point in looking like a hag beside him. Raoul was considered an excellent catch. And as long as people were going to gossip, she might as well enjoy the benefit of a few compliments as well as the usual catty remarks. She hooked on strands of jade over the beige dress and added earrings and bracelet to match. A tiny throb began to tap in her temples. Ellen recognized that it was a manifestation of fear. She was afraid of Raoul. She was concerned about what he might do to her tonight.

Raoul knew that Ellen could not fight against the tantilizing bait of sexual contact. Another woman might be able to play his game and laugh at Raoul. But Ellen had no other outlets for her frustration. Raoul knew this and could therefore take advantage. He could manipulate Ellen to his own whims. If Ellen had any courage at all, she would tell Raoul to go away right now. But a stupid hope was compelling her to go out with him. And the hope was that Jay would see them together.

Ellen went with Raoul into Sandy's automobile. But he did not drive in the direction of the country club or to any of the places of entertainment she knew.

They drove for almost a half hour without saying a word to each other. Ellen's curiosity had begun to grow as they rode through the center of town and out onto the highway. She looked up to the clouds taking on a glow of moonlight and watched the trees whip past them as the car took on speed.

"All right," Ellen said at last. "I give in. Where are we going?"

"Surprise," Raoul said. "You'll see when we get there." He sounded pleased with himself and confident that Ellen would be pleased with him too.

He turned off the main road and the car wound up a narrow pathway into the hills. She had never come along this particular route before. Naked branches overhung the road with twisted, intermingling arms. Piles of leaves were drifted across the lane and the wheels crunched over them, making sharp cracking sounds as they ran over an occasional twig.

Ellen's fear became tinged with a pointed curiosity. She felt caught in a cage with a hungry lion and the fear had something dreadfully appealing about it. Raoul stopped the car in what seemed to be the middle of nowhere. He could murder her, Ellen realized. Her body would not be found for months. He helped her out of the car and she heard something gallop away through the trees.

"Deer," Raoul said as she looked with alarm in the direction of the sound. "Come along."

She followed him carefully over upturned roots of trees. A sword of lightning had once upon a time cut this twisted path through the wood. They came out into a small clearing where a cabin stood alone beneath the drifting moon.

Raoul pushed the door open and took Ellen into a cozy room with polished floors and a potbellied stove which gave off warmth and the odor of pine. Someone had cleaned the place recently because no dust or cobwebs disturbed the rustic comfort. A wide cot with maroon blankets pulled hospital tight stood against one wall.

"Was it worth the ride?" Raoul said.

Ellen didn't know. The place was certainly inviting. But how would Raoul treat her now that they were really alone?

"Let me have your coat," he said.

Ellen sat down in a high backed rocker and waited for Raoul's next move. She had no intention of throwing herself at him. But her nerves were not at all placid. Twinges of expectancy niggled at her outward calm. She waited to see what Raoul would do next.

He set a pan of something on the stove, then took two mugs from the small cupboard.

"It's wonderful up here," he said. "No crowds, no secretaries running out of type cleaner. I rented this cabin until December. If we're lucky, it won't snow too hard before then."

Ellen gazed at Raoul and thought how strange they both looked in this little hunter's cabin. They were dressed for chic night life or the privacy of a hotel suite. But like two culprits, here they hid on the side of a mountain.

"This was very romantic of you," she said, considering it to be the best compliment for him.

"Hardly," Raoul smiled. "The word is practical. The odds against getting you to New York seemed intolerably high."

"Very true," Ellen smiled in turn. "Once a country girl, always a country girl."

"I wonder."

He poured the liquid into the mugs and shook cinnamon into them. "Try this."

Ellen took a sip but she couldn't figure out what the ingredients were. The drink had a spicy taste reminiscent of cappucino, but there was some kind of alcohol too. "Rum?"

"Partly. That's something the cave men used to drink before going out to hunt down a woman."

Ellen finished most of the drink. The piquant taste appealed to her and stimulated her into higher spirits. She felt a growing sense of adventure and followed Raoul's movements as he stretched out on the cot, hoping he would beckon her to come to him. She felt carefree. Her body, dropping its pose of inhibition, began to tingle in secret places. And she knew that Raoul would not get away from her tonight.

She watched him finish his drink and set the mug down on the Indian rug beside him. "How're we doing?" she said.

"Fine. Why don't you come join me?"

Ellen didn't need to be coaxed. She went to the bed and lay down beside Raoul. She could feel the tension in the muscles of his legs beneath his trousers. Slowly her body began massaging itself against Raoul's. Tentacles of desire clutched and clung to the insides of her thighs. She ran a forefinger around the outline of his mouth. "Thank you for the roses," she said.

He took her fingers and held them still so that he could kiss their tips. "You're very welcome."

His hands slid up the length of her arms and played with the necklace. "Are you warm enough?" he said.

"Too warm." Ellen reached behind her neck, took off the necklace and dropped it into his palm. "Put those in your pocket for me."

"You do that."

The creaking of branches outside accompanied the clinking sound as Ellen slipped the jade into his handkerchief pocket. She wasn't going to wait for Raoul to make the decisions. Systematically she pushed off one shoe, then the other. As Raoul watched she slowly took off all her clothes and stood naked before him on the rug.

"Did I thank you for the roses?" she said and leaned over him so that her nipples grazed across his mouth. Before he could grasp them, she stood up again.

"Yes, you thanked me," he answered with a smirk that acknowledged Ellen's motives. "As long as you're up, would you like to take my jacket?"

"Certainly." She stood just out of reach while Raoul handed her first his jacket, then his tie and shirt, his trousers, then his underwear. She had never seen him completely undressed before and Ellen realized what she had missed. He wasn't a massive man, but his muscles were well-knit and solidly packed against his sturdy frame.

"You're very beautiful," Ellen said. She was acting with a wisdom not her own. Perhaps the rum in the drink was guiding her with Raoul.

"Come here and show me that you mean it." His soft straight hair had fallen over his forehead, disturbing the aura of cold control which had been Ellen's fear.

She went to the cot and lay herself full length on top of him. She felt their legs intertwine and the presence of Raoul's nails digging into the flesh of her back. His lips sought out her earlobe, the curve of her neck, the yearning breasts. Ellen clung to him fiercely, knowing that Raoul would not escape her now.

Raoul turned her onto her back. His lips caught one hard nipple. The movement of his tongue goaded her into shuddering points of desire.

"Touch me," he said. "Really touch me."

The palm of her hand slid down below his stomach. Slowly she massaged him. In expectation her hips began a swaying movement. He began to insinuate himself between her moist thighs.

"Not yet," she murmured, wanting to prolong the delicious agony.

Instinctively her arms pulled him tighter. She felt her breasts flatten against the soft hairs of his chest. An urge to bite overwhelmed her. She caught a bit of flesh between her teeth and nipped it, playfully yet voraciously. The damp odor of his skin came pungently to her nostrils.

"Now?" he said.

"Umm." Her tone was tremulous.

Ellen stiffened as she felt the sudden ecstacy of contact. Waves of contraction gripped her lower belly. Her legs tightened around him.

"Harder ... harder, damn you."

The thrust and pull sent waves of thrill through her. The world spun far away. She was part of another, more primitive world which knew only desire and gratification. She plunged wildly onward. In rivulets of perspiration, her skin clung damply to his.

Her craving, like a great strong animal, leaped in a high wide arc across a spaceless chasm. She shuddered for a fleeting second. Then her body went limp. A smile spread lazily across her lips.

Finally the embers in the little Franklin stove crackled and died. When Raoul took her home, Ellen slept peacefully like a creature new born.

Ellen was possessed. Whether Raoul was good for her or not, she knew she would be with him every weekend for as long as he wanted her. Three months until the end of December. She wouldn't worry about afterward until the time came.

She saw Jay on Saturday as she had promised. But afterward she met Raoul and they went up to the mountain again. They spent Sunday afternoon in the cabin too. Ellen flung herself into an orgy of fulfillment, knowing that she would have to spend Monday through Thursday alone. Afraid that Raoul might cool toward her, she tried to prevent him from achieving complete satisfaction. But she could never succeed in doing this. With him, all thought of tomorrow was lost and she flogged their bodies on to greater and greater heights of passion.

During the week Ellen avoided Jay. The contrast of Raoul's driving lust with Jay's plodding manner made her impatient with his talk about children and his immature efforts to please her. Ellen ate well and slept peacefully and spent the evenings being a happy companion to her son.

Raoul continued to send flowers and the house became a veritable bouquet of love. On the surface, Ellen was content. As long as she didn't think beyond the moment, she was satisfied.

The days became shorter as winter tightened its grip on the earth. Each weekend they brewed and drank deeply from the cup of love. Raoul taught Ellen pleasures she had never known before. Strange titillating experiences that made ecstasy a maze of unending pleasures. Ellen gained a few pounds and the hollows in her cheeks filled out. The whiskey bottles in her bar at home remained untouched.

One Tuesday night, Jay brought Warrie home and Ellen invited him in because it was the polite gesture to make.

Jay had lost the casual manner which had originally inspired Ellen's interest. He waited for her to ask him before he took a seat in the living room. Doreen had fixed a light supper for Warrie and they heard the refrigerator door slam as he took something extra to go with his meal.

"You know, I've been up to my ears in work," Jay said. "I guess it's my fault that we haven't been seeing much of each other lately."

She felt sorry for Jay. He looked bewildered and unhappy about the rift in their relationship. But Ellen had given Jay his chance. If anything, she had given him more than the usual chance to encourage their relationship.

"I hope school is going along well," Ellen said. It was kinder to talk about Jay's work instead of themselves. "This was the first time in I don't know how long that it was a pleasure to sign Warrie's report card. You're a wonderful person, Jay."

"We should manage to see more of each other somehow." His voice did not have quite so much confidence. "Let's go to a movie tonight. That is, if you're not busy."

Would it be wise to lead Jay on?

"There's an old Hepburn picture playing at the Mayfax. How about it, Ellen?"

He looked at her so lost, so unsure. It couldn't do any harm to spend an evening with him. "Yes," she said. "I think that would be fun."

She saw the dimple come into his cheek. It only showed when he smiled deeply and with true happiness. She was glad.

Warrie came in, still chewing the last morsel of his supper. "Did I hear movies?" he said.

"Not for you," Jay replied. "I'm taking your mother tonight. She deserves some time off."

"She goes out more than I do," Warrie said, protruding his lips with a pout of disappointment.

"Well," Jay hesitated. "That's good."

"It's good for everybody except me. I hate school."

"No you don't," Ellen said. She saw Warrie look at Jay challengingly. But Jay knew better than to argue. He had Warrie in complete control and didn't need to squash this minor rebellion with a platitude.

"We'll be home early," Jay said. "That's a promise."

Warrie made the sound of an old man's sigh and accepted defeat because Jay gave him no alternative.

Ellen had never ridden in Jay's car. The old vehicle clattered, jounced, emphasizing bumps that Ellen didn't know existed in the road.

The small theater had only a scattering of people and they took seats in the last row. At first they sat and watched the film, munching popcorn from the large bagful on Jay's lap. Then she felt his arm steal around the back of her chair. She thought it better not to make a fuss and appeared to ignore the touch of his hand on her shoulder.

Afterward he took her to a luncheonette and ordered coffee and danish.

"I never saw that picture," Ellen said, searching for conversation. "She certainly looked young, didn't she?"

"How about a real date with me this Saturday? We'll go dancing and the works."

"No, Jay, not this Saturday. I'm sorry."

"Friday night then?"

She didn't know how to get around his persistence. She couldn't very well tell him that her weekends would never be free. Raoul had not committed himself about anything except their sexual communion. Even if Raoul had asked her to marry him, Ellen wasn't sure that she would accept. He wasn't the kind of a man she wanted to have for Warrie's father. Besides, marriage to Raoul would mean moving to New York. It wouldn't be fair to Warrie to disrupt him now that he was finally beginning to straighten himself out. Yet she was not prepared to give up Raoul. She had no confidence in Jay as an adequate lover. And love was doing wonders for her. Perhaps she shouldn't call it love. Satiety was doing wonders for her.

"You're busy Friday *and* Saturday," Jay said to her.

"I'm afraid so."

"Sunday too, I suspect." He wiped his fingers on a napkin, crumpled it into a ball and dropped it into the cup.

"Yes," Ellen said flatly. "But that leaves Monday, Tuesday, Wednesday and Thursday."

"You forget swimming classes, scout meetings and remedial instruction."

"But you managed to get out tonight." She motioned to the waiter for another cup of coffee. As long as they were sitting in a public booth, their argument couldn't become overly heated. If they were alone in the car, they might come to sharp words.

"I purposely took off tonight because we haven't been seeing each other. But I can't do this very often. I shouldn't have done it this evening."

Their conversation stopped while the waiter placed second cups for them both. A group of teenagers had come in and were dawdling about the counter. One of them passed their table to drop coins into the juke box. An old Benny Goodman record sent forth a lively clarinet melody.

"Don't you want us to see each other?" Jay said.

"Of course I do." This was the truth. She could afford to like Jay now that she didn't need him to exert evidence of his manhood. They could have a pleasant friendship. Maybe go sleigh riding when the snows came. Ordinarily Ellen looked forward to the hills massed in white. But now snow meant that she and Raoul could not reach the cabin. Already it was the end of October. She wondered when Raoul would mention something to her about what they were going to do.

"I don't know what to think," Jay said. "We seemed to be doing so well and now you're a changed person. What is it, Ellen? Has something gone wrong that I should know about?"

She couldn't very well tell him that something had suddenly gone right. "Time, Jay. We need time, that's all."

She stood up and walked to the door, allowing him no choice but to pay the check and take her home.

In the car Jay tried to cover his confusion with humorous anecdotes about the swimming class. Ellen tried to listen attentively, but she just didn't care about who fell in at the shallow end and thought he was drowning.

Jay braked in front of her house and leaned over to try to kiss her. Ellen tried not to notice his action and opened the door and got out. She didn't invite him inside.

"I'll call you," he said with a floundering voice.

"Yes, do that."

Ellen hurried inside without looking back.

The movie had let out at nine thirty. It was now only an hour later and Warrie was sitting up in bed waiting for her. He had a model airplane on the blanket and was making engine noises with his lips.

"Hi there," Ellen said. "Still up?"

"Come on in," Warrie said. "I want to talk to you anyway."

Ellen opened her coat and rushes of cold air emanated from the folds. She sat down on the edge of Warrie's bed and rubbed her hands on the warm quilt. "What do you want to talk to me about?"

"I just wanted to ask you a question." He looped the plane upward and landed it on the night table.

Ellen waited, concerned that Warrie was going to speak on Jay's behalf. He must have noticed that the three of them were not functioning as a unit anymore. Maybe he understood that something had changed.

"Who is that man you go out with all the time?" Warrie said bluntly.

Ellen felt herself stiffen. She wasn't aware that Warrie placed any importance on her weekend socializing. He himself was so busy with outings and boy scout meetings that she thought he wouldn't bother about her activities.

"I watched you from the window but I don't know who he is."

Ellen wasn't sure how she would cope with this situation. Supposing she introduced Raoul to Warrie. If Warrie took a disliking to him, it might cause complications. But if Raoul might be seriously thinking about marrying her, Warrie should meet and get to know him better.

"His name is Raoul Verne," Ellen said casually. "He's a very nice man from New York."

"If he's from New York, what's he doing here all the time?"

"He visits his sister." She could tell that Warrie wasn't particularly upset about her going out with Raoul. A natural childish curiosity had prompted his questioning.

"I think he visits you," Warrie said with a huge smile that accused Raoul of being a sissy.

"He visits both of us. Would you like to meet him?" She wanted Warrie to feel included in her activities.

"Nope." He wiggled down under the covers and pulled them up to his nose.

Ellen knew that he was satisfied now that she wasn't trying to keep any secrets from him. She kissed him on the forehead, switched out the lights and went out.

This incident stirred Ellen to face her situation squarely. She had been avoiding any plans about the future with Raoul. Often he told Ellen how much he wanted her. But their lovemaking did not include the tenderer side of passion which might give her the confidence to hope for a marriage. Except for sex, their interests were completely divergent. Raoul functioned in a world unknown to her. Ellen was not sure that she wanted to become part of that world. Something definite would have to happen between them. She would work hard at the job of being a good wife to Raoul. But the idea didn't satisfy her. Ellen missed something in their relationship. They reached out for each other's bodies but there was between them no deeper communion than that of the flesh. This weekend, she would try to investigate further and discover what Raoul and she really meant to each other.

Ellen was in the process of cleaning Warrie's hiking boots one afternoon when the doorbell rang and Nita came in. She opened her Hudson seal coat but did not take it off.

"Would you like to come with me to the hospital?" she said. "I'm going to pick up Charles and Dick Wayne."

Ellen could tell that Nita had something on her mind besides just a casual trip. "Isn't he supposed to be in Paris by now?" Ellen asked. She put down the boots and wiped her hands on the cloth.

"He was disappointed in the job out there. So he came back to the states. Dick is a fast worker, you know."

The two women hadn't seen each other since the first night Ellen had gone with Raoul. But Nita didn't make any of the conventional inquiries about where she had been or what was keeping her so busy. Ellen felt an impulse to confide in her, but she restrained it. Maybe Nita wasn't interested.

"So Dr. Wayne is at the hospital working with Charles?"

"Yes, but I don't know for how long. Anyway, he asked for you. And since you seemed so curious about him, I thought this would be a good time for all of us to get together. You haven't seen my husband recently either. I'm sure you'd like to reestablish acquaintance with Charles."

Nita's manner was a little stiff and Ellen recalled the letter she had sent.

"Yes," Ellen said. "I'd like to go with you." She washed her hands and put on the dark mink which she wore in extremely cold weather during the day. It was tailored for afternoon dress and did not seem at all out of place with the heavy gloves and a bright kerchief around her head.

"I've missed you, Nita. Why haven't you called?"

"You could have called."

This was true and Ellen knew that only shame and guilt had prevented her. "To be honest," Ellen said, "I was a little hesitant after that night. I made a fool of myself. And I'm not even sure that I remember everything I did."

"I hoped you would have forgotten about that by now. We all have our moments."

In this swift moment, Ellen felt complete forgiveness. She had magnified the situation. Nita thought nothing of it.

"Thank you for taking the initiative today," Ellen said softly and went with Nita to her Lincoln.

The large green car suited Nita's appearance. It had just the right amount of elegance and dash.

"I've been thinking about you," Nita said. "You have an odd kind of innocence for a grown woman."

"That's a delusion," Ellen replied. Nita simply didn't know what Ellen had been doing with her weekends. "If anything, I'm an immoral slut." She laughed as she said the words because Ellen knew that Nita wouldn't believe them.

"You keep that well hidden."

Once again they were into the old swing of conversation and Ellen realized how much she had missed it. She didn't talk very much with Raoul. They had nothing to say to each other. Oh, she prodded him to tell her about divorce cases, but he didn't seem inclined to enjoy dwelling on what he did all week. And what could Ellen tell him except the boring details of keeping a home. She didn't want to speak of her son because that would tacitly mention Warren.

"If I told you all the things I've been doing," Ellen said, "your hair would stand right up and raise the roof off the car."

"Too cold for that," Nita said. "Better not tell me."

Yet Ellen felt an irresistible desire to tell her. She needed another woman to confide in. Somebody who would be objective and sympathetic too. Maybe Nita could give her some advice.

"May I tell you?" Ellen asked.

"If you won't regret it."

The sentence gave Ellen pause. She certainly didn't want to lower herself any further in Nita's eyes.

"I knew that would stop you," Nita laughed. The black coat made her look very soft. Ellen remembered the sensation she had felt upon seeing the woman naked. And back into her mind slipped the recollection of falling asleep in Nita's arms. These memories made her uncertain. She wondered if Nita considered her strange in any way. She must tell her something about Raoul.

"You'll be glad to hear," she began, "that I haven't been seeing much of Jay Masters lately. In fact I haven't seen him at all in more than a week."

"Very encouraging," Nita said. The pigskin gloves drew across the backs of her hands as she swerved the wheel of the car. Everything about her seemed less than serious. Ellen wondered if she were capable of shocking Nita.

"Do you know the Vernes?" Ellen asked. She heard a wicked laugh proceed from Nita's throat.

"I used to know Sandra Verne quite well," she said. "We haven't seen each other in years, though. I don't think she would want to see me either."

This surprised Ellen. She thought that Sandy could get on with just about anybody. And Nita certainly wasn't that hard to take.

"Then perhaps you know Sandy's brother, Raoul?"

"No, I never met him."

Ellen felt disappointed. "I wish you had," she said. She cleared the vapor off from the side window and stared at the frozen earth. There really was no use in giving away her secret. Whatever would happen between Raoul and herself would have to remain a private matter.

Nita did not press her for further details. She allowed Ellen to lapse into her own thoughts until they reached the low building situated midway between two towns.

Their footsteps resounded overloud in the hospital corridor. Nita took Ellen into a large office with DR. PROBISH painted on the door. Two walls of the room were lined with books. A snapshot of Joey poked out from the blotter of the old desk.

"Make yourself at home," Nita said lighting a cigarette. "We're ten minutes early."

Ellen sat down in the sunken leather reading chair. She could imagine Charles engrossed here until late at night with one of the volumes from the shelves. She watched Nita place herself in the swivel chair and swing around to face the window.

"This is such a cooped up room," Nita said. "I don't know how he can stand it."

Ellen thought it was a very comfortable place, not at all tiny. A sense of organization ruled here. The many papers were stacked in neat folders on the desktop. The rug wasn't very worn though the chair she was sitting in was apparently well used. She could almost feel Charles' contemplative presence dominating.

Ten minutes came and went. The door opened and Richard Wayne entered. He held a pair of rubber gloves and the rest of him was almost completely covered by the white hospital uniform. Ellen thought he looked rather dignified.

"Sorry to keep you waiting," he said to Nita. Then he noticed Ellen and he took the white cap off his head, revealing wavy brown hair that Ellen didn't remember to be so thick. "Mrs. Tendler," he said. "I thought Nita had forgotten to convey my message."

Ellen extended her hand and he gripped it firmly.

He had none of Raoul's flash nor the athletic masculinity of Jay. But she detected something else in the handshake. A sureness, a dependability. Ellen knew that patients would feel confident in his care. She wondered what the message was that Nita was supposed to give her. Perhaps simply that Richard Wayne would like to see her again. And Nita had told her this.

"I'll just get my things and we can go," he said. "You folks will bear with me for a minute?"

"Of course," Ellen said.

He went out again and Ellen said to Nita, "I'm sorry we have to miss Charles."

"Don't be," Nita replied. "This is nothing unusual."

Ellen felt that Nita had managed to make a deal with her loneliness. She realized that Charles gave only the leftovers of himself to his home.

"Will you forget about that letter? I have a big mouth and a small brain."

Nita stubbed out her cigarette. "I'll make a bargain with you, Ellen. I'll forget that letter if you'll forget about that night I stayed with you."

There was an urgency in Nita's voice that Ellen could not account for. Nita hadn't done anything to require forgiveness. On the contrary, she had been generous and helpful. Ellen looked at her quizzically.

"Sometimes," Nita said, "things happen that one doesn't plan. I had no intention of…"

Richard Wayne came back in. He was dressed in a dark brown suit that complimented his hair. As he smiled, Ellen forgot the thick glasses and saw only the depth of hazel eyes behind them.

"Let's have dinner out," Richard said. "You've earned a vacation from domestic slavery, Nita. We'll go to Ruggio's and relax you." He turned to Ellen. "Has Nita told you that I'm practically living at her house?"

"He's been with us for two weeks now," Nita explained. "And I think he's tired of my cooking."

Nita drove and Ellen sat between them as they continued to the town on the other side of the hospital. She knew the Italian restaurant. It was a large place with a quiet orchestra which didn't intrude itself on those who preferred not to dance.

Richard ordered for the three of them and danced with Nita and Ellen in turn. He had the ability to doff preoccupation with medical research and enjoy himself socially.

"I was beginning to lose hope," he said to Ellen as they circled the dance floor. "Tried to reach you last Saturday and the Sunday afternoon before that. Have you got a secret hiding place or am I dancing with the most popular woman in town?"

"Both," Ellen grinned. But behind her laughter, she felt a strange twinge of conscience. Dick Wayne was a good dancer and Ellen didn't feel that this was a waste of time as it would be with Raoul.

"Nita tells me you didn't enjoy your stay in Paris," Ellen said, wanting to switch the conversation away from herself.

"Disappointing. They don't have enough facilities for the enzyme research we're doing. Charles offered me full speed ahead in his laboratory. So I'll be trying that out for awhile."

"You're not here permanently, then?" Ellen said.

"No. I have until the end of the month to decide. There's a research center in Washington that interests me. I may go there."

Ellen didn't comment. She thought it would be fun to go out with Dick once in awhile.

They returned to the table and found Nita pouring chianti. The special antipasto of stuffed mushrooms and eggplant put Ellen in a festival mood. She was glad to be out in the open for a change. Sneaking up to the cabin had taken its toll. Something healthy about tonight contrasted with the sordidness of her relationship to Raoul.

She ate veal scallopini with zest and accepted an Italian pastry not caring about its overabundance of calories. The hours flew by quickly and Ellen was sorry to go home. Ellen wished she could spend a few private minutes with Nita and finish their interrupted conversation.

The next evening she phoned Nita, planning to invite her over to find out just what had happened. But Richard answered the telephone and he came over instead. Ellen didn't mind. She enjoyed the change of face around the house.

Warrie came in, took one look at Richard, and said, "Who's this one?"

Richard extended his hand man to man. "I'm Dick Wayne, sir. Who are you?"

He looked at the hand, then up the long distance to Richard's face. "I'm Warren Edward Tendler," he answered seriously.

Ellen watched the little hand clasp the huge one. She saw her son standing very straight and thought how he would look ten years from now, as tall as Richard.

"Excuse me, Mr. Wayne. I have to get my gym shorts."

"Dr. Wayne," Ellen interrupted.

Warrie turned to her. "Are you sick again?"

"No," she replied. "Dr. Wayne is a friend."

"Well, excuse me."

When Warrie had left them, Dick said, "Everybody hates a doctor."

"Not at all. I'm surprised and pleased to say that I think you won him over with that courtly exhibition."

"Doesn't he like many people?"

Because Richard was in the medical profession, he would understand. "He's just about getting over the death of his father. It's been quite a struggle."

"He's a good kid, Ellen. I hope you don't worry about him."

"Let's go for a walk," she said. Ellen needed to be out in the wintry night. She didn't want to get involved with Richard Wayne. Serious conversation would lead to interest. Then interest to involvement. She had enough to deal with Raoul. Ellen could foresee Richard trying to make an appointment with her for some weekend. Either she would have to brush him off completely or give him some good reason why not. Neither of these could she do with honesty.

They went out into the night and battled a few blocks of the wind. Then he brought her home again, but did not try to invite himself in. She knew that Richard perceived her desire to keep their relationship impersonal.

When Raoul called for her that Friday, Ellen decided that the time had come for her to talk about their situation in more definite terms. She waited until they had reached the cabin before saying anything.

After Raoul shut the door, he didn't give her a chance to talk. He grabbed her and shut the words off with kisses. Though her intentions had been good, Ellen succumbed to his desire. Still completely dressed, they reached the cot and fell down on it together. Savagely he tore at her clothes and she responded with an equal lust. The needs of her mind went dead before the greater craving of her body. They didn't bother about the formalities of pre-play. No spicy drinks. No teasing each other with words. Each knew what the other wanted and they slaked their thirst at the fountain of fulfillment.

When Ellen finally came away from him, her thoughts were disorganized. She wanted to sleep in his arms and forget about tomorrow. But she had to speak.

"It's almost the middle of November," she said.

Raoul turned over on his stomach and closed his eyes. "Um hmm."

"Then it will be the end of the month," she continued.

Raoul's lids had closed in sleep. She knew better than to wake him. He would agree to anything she said only to be left alone.

Ellen tried again Saturday and Sunday. Each time she was defeated by the animal needs of her body. When he drove her home Sunday evening, Ellen said "I don't think we'll be seeing each other next week."

"Why not?"

How could she put it to him when the idea was so unformed in her own mind. "I think we're taking up too much of each other's time," she said.

"Nonsense." They were parked in front of her house and anybody could drive by and see them.

"Why don't you come inside and we'll talk about it?" Ellen offered.

"There's nothing to discuss." His mood was definite.

"Raoul, do you realize we haven't said a word to each other about anything except … You know what I mean."

He rolled up the window beside him and leaned his elbow on the steering wheel. "That's what I like about us," he said. "We don't use useless words. I understand you and you understand me. Let's leave the words for litigation."

But he didn't understand her. Raoul understood only what pleased him. He didn't want to see that there was more to a relationship than two people hopping in and out of bed with each other.

"Raoul, let's face it. We can't go on this way. Pretty soon we won't be able to get up to the cabin."

"Oh, that's what's bothering you. Well, don't worry. I'm going to make arrangements for you to come into the city."

"But I don't want to come in to the city. All this makes me feel like an animal. I'm tired of it. I don't want the cabin or hotels or anything. Can't you understand?"

"Yes. But I don't believe you. Now it's getting late. I have to catch the train."

"Don't call for me next Friday."

"All right." He had a vicious smile on his lips. "But you'll be sorry."

Ellen slammed out of the car and ran inside. No, she wouldn't be sorry. If Raoul wanted her, he'd have to make other arrangements than treating her like a part time mistress. She wouldn't be sorry at all not to see him next weekend.

But she became increasingly nervous as the week went by. Her body had become accustomed to regular satisfaction. She remembered her suffering before Raoul returned into her life. To go through that again would be slow suicide. Ellen sat by the telephone and wished someone would call her. She had maneuvered herself into an unstrategic position. All the people she knew took for granted that her weekends were reserved. Jay wouldn't call.

Dick wouldn't call. Ellen realized that she had condemned herself to three days of miserable solitude.

But she refused to get in touch with Raoul. She wasn't going to become his slave. When Friday night arrived, Ellen took a cold shower and tried to go to sleep early. The bed felt like a mattress full of stones and she turned and twisted through the night haunted by the call of her desire, which echoed through her flesh like a demon ghost.

The dawn stole across the sky and Ellen went to make herself a pot of black coffee. Her body had established its own routine of desire and satisfaction. Now it battled against her traitorous negation and she shivered with overwhelming need.

Warrie was up and out of the house early. She had nobody to talk to, nothing to take her mind off the violent urges which would not allow her a moment's peace.

Saturday night came and Ellen hadn't gotten dressed yet. She had no reason to put on clothes. She felt like a sick one. Passion ate away her reserves of energy. She couldn't stand another night alone. The waking nightmare of her solitude disrupted Ellen's rational thinking. She went to the phone and prayed that Nita would come keep her company.

An hour later Nita arrived. She took one look at Ellen and went to make her something to eat. Ellen followed after her like a dog.

"What's the matter with you, girl?" Nita sounded honestly concerned.

"I don't know," Ellen said. She really didn't know. Any normal person could control the natural instincts. If she couldn't, something must be terribly wrong.

She tried to eat the chicken soup and managed to get half of it down. "I'm so grateful to you for coming over. You don't know how much I need you, Nita. There has never been anyone so good to me as you are." A passionate tremor reverberated in her voice.

She looked up at Nita and grasped the woman by both wrists. "You're like an angel from heaven."

"Let's not go overboard with this," Nita smiled. "After all, I don't exactly dislike you either." She looked at the bowl. "Now finish your soup."

Ellen forced the rest of it down. Anything Nita told her to do, she would do gladly.

"Have you slept at all?" Nita said. She took the bowl and washed it out.

"No. But I'll sleep tonight. It's easier to sleep when you're not alone. Something about you gives me the courage to sleep." She looked at the complete calmness of Nita with admiration. The cashmere sweater and skirt added a businesslike attitude to her manner. Ellen wished that Nita would command her to sleep.

For awhile Nita diverted Ellen's attention with small talk about clothes. Ellen felt herself becoming interested in stories about various designers Nita had met in Europe. When ten o'clock came, she felt completely exhausted.

"I hope it isn't too early for you," Ellen said.

Nita steered her into the bedroom. "We'll see."

Ellen climbed in and waited for her friend. She watched Nita undress and wished she owned some of the woman's lovely perfume. "Are you sure you don't want a gown?"

"No thanks. I prefer sleeping raw. Goodness knows it's warm enough in here." She got in and stayed on the far edge of the bed.

"Do you have enough room?"

"Plenty. Shut your eyes."

Ellen shut her eyes but they wouldn't stay closed. She felt drowsy, but not enough to drift off. And she felt Nita fully awake beside her. It would be selfish to go to sleep and leave her friend alone. Ellen turned on her side facing Nita.

"Why do you hate men?" she said. No thought had prompted the question. It seemed to have popped into Ellen's mind from the deep well of her subconscious.

"That's not a question for bedtime," Nita's voice was very soft in the darkness.

Ellen could sense the distance between them. She didn't want Nita to lie so far away from her. She wanted to reach out and touch the smoothness of her body. A physical contact with someone else might ease the remembrance of Raoul. Ellen's hand crept forward until it found Nita's. She held it firmly so that Nita could not pull away.

"You're not trying to sleep," Nita said.

"I'm afraid you'd fall off the bed. I wish you'd move in." Ellen didn't know what she wanted. Vaguely she remembered how it felt to sleep in Nita's arms but she felt ashamed to try it now. If she had the excuse of being drunk, it would be easier. An expanse of emptiness seemed to widen in her heart as she realized that she could not decently force herself on Nita's attention. She must settle for the beggarly contact of their fingers. Yet she yearned for something greater.

Then she felt Nita's body moving closer. She dared not hope that the woman would take her in her arms.

"Would you like a nightcap?" Ellen said.

"No thanks. Close your mouth and go to sleep."

"One drink." The idea seemed wonderful. Before Nita could protest, Ellen swung out of bed and returned with a bottle and two glasses. She filled them both generously.

"You don't know what you're doing," Nita said. She would not touch a drop of her own, but set the glass down on the night table.

Ellen finished her drink, turning from Nita so she could not take the glass away from her.

"There," she said triumphantly. "Now I can sleep." She knew she was being childish. But something impelled her. She needed to relax and whiskey always untied her nerves.

Ellen got back into bed and drew a sigh of relief. "My, that feels strange on an almost empty stomach," she breathed.

"You're playing a dangerous game, Ellen," Nita said seriously.

Oh, she knew that this was the way people started out to be alcoholics. But the thought didn't really worry her. If she was doomed to that fate, it would have taken over during the three years of becoming accustomed to Warren's death.

"Don't worry about me," she said and smiled in the darkness. A window pane out in the hall rattled. With a sudden unthinking action, she snuggled close to Nita. "We're good friends, aren't we?"

"Yes," Nita said.

"How good?" Ellen asked. She needed reassurance, she needed affection, she needed attention.

"All right, Ellen," Nita sighed. A gate of reserve seemed to give way with her words. She put her arms around Ellen's back and lifted her upward. Nita's lips pressed onto hers and Ellen felt Nita's breasts blend with her own breasts in a sudden release of passionate desire.

Automatically Ellen pulled Nita even closer. The craving in her body knew only that its satisfaction was within reach.

Gladly Ellen yielded to the soft yet strangely demanding caress. Her mind, fogged with whiskey, did not bother to question. She knew only that Nita wanted her, needed her. And that she herself wanted and needed in return.

The point of Nita's tongue moved smoothly and moistly down the side of Ellen's neck. The woman's lips lingered in the hollow of her throat and Ellen tilted her head back, enchanted by the exotic fragrance of perfume. She ran her fingers through Nita's soft hair and her palm settled on the warm temple. She felt the throbbing pulse. Her own senses throbbed in response. Soon Nita's lips wandered downward, seeking and finding the curve of Ellen's breast, then the intimate pocket of skin beneath her bosom.

"I've wanted you ..." Nita murmured, but the rest of her thought dissolved as her mouth circled around Ellen's stomach.

Nita's hands went beneath Ellen's hips and lifted them. Willingly Ellen yielded herself. She did not know, she did not care what happened so long as she could find release from the demon in her loins. She felt the softness of Nita's cheek against her thigh. Then the world began to rock as she drowned in sensation.

"Hurt me." Her voice, low and rasping, sounded like a stranger's.

Ellen's back arched tautly. Her breasts shuddered and she clenched her teeth almost unable to bear the mounting pleasure.

"So good … so good."

Then her fingers tightened in Nita's hair. Her body became like a rocket as it seemed to burst and shower down in fast falling sparks of release.

The cold night roared outside, enraged with its own bitterness. Nita's kisses had dissolved all sound, all unrest and Ellen gave of herself in a final spasm of ecstasy.

Afterward they lay together and Ellen's mind refused to comprehend what had transpired. In this moment of peacefulness, she knew only that Nita had saved her from the addiction to Raoul. Her body felt weighted with a desire for sleep. Without question she put a cheek against Nita's breast and drifted into burdenless dreaming.

When she awoke, Nita was still clinging to her. She lifted her head and saw Nita still fast asleep. For awhile she listened to the gentle breathing, then slowly recollected their union. She moved quietly away from Nita and looked down at her own body with increasingly troubled thoughts.

Ellen had no doubt that she had been completely sated. But she was not a man hater. She looked again at Nita and discovered nothing masculine about the rounded shoulders or sloping breasts. Yet they had managed to appease each other without the need for men. Was this the answer to her problem with Raoul?

Could she escape the trap of desire by indulging herself with Nita?

Ellen's thoughts were on unfamiliar ground. She wanted to waken Nita and question her. Nita had known what she was doing last night. Undoubtedly she had shared this experience with other women. If Nita indulged herself this way, it couldn't be wrong. But these thoughts did not please Ellen. She went into the bathroom and took a hot shower.

By the time she came out again, Nita had awakened. "You slept well," she said.

"Yes." Ellen came over and sat down on the bed. She didn't want to hurt Nita's feelings, but she couldn't accept their experience together as though she were accustomed to it. "I know it was all my fault," Ellen began. "I forced myself on you."

"Let's not have any blame or praise," Nita said. "Now that you know what happens when you're drunk, perhaps you won't invite me to stay over with you quite so often." There was no anger in her voice or self-contempt.

"Has it happened before with us?"

"Well, not that completely," Nita admitted. "You needed someone last night. I happened to be here. Don't start calling yourself dirty names. Let me assure you from past experience, my dear, that you are a very normal woman. Sex knows no roles when it's searching with so much zeal. Just say to yourself beggars can't be choosers and let it go at that." She smiled with a generosity that put Ellen to shame.

"I won't be able to forget it," Ellen said. "Nor do I want to."

"But it doesn't solve your problem. I understand." Nita got out of bed, and Ellen looked at the body which had been hers a mere few hours ago.

"This won't break up our friendship?" Ellen asked. She adored Nita but there was an extra facet to being in love which no woman could ever fulfill.

"Of course not. I'm thankful that you're not cursing me."

A tide of sadness came over Ellen. Why should she curse something that had saved her in a moment of need? She had brought the experience on. What's more, she had enjoyed it completely for what it could give her. To curse Nita would only make herself a hypocrite.

There wasn't much left to say. Ellen provided Nita with a towel and turned on the shower faucets for her.

Afterward Ellen explained to her all about Raoul. There was no more need for secrecy. Nita listened attentively to Ellen's story. A better friendship had come as the result of their experience together. For this alone Ellen could be grateful.

But Nita's advice about Raoul was something Ellen knew she could not manage. Had not this weekend demonstrated how much she needed someone? She knew she could not go without some promise of sexual easement from a definite and dependable source. Besides it was not only a question of physicality. She needed to build another home for her son.

"I don't know," Nita admitted. "We'll have to think this over carefully."

After she left, Ellen reviewed her experience. She wondered if it would be a terrible thing to go to Nita until she had escaped Raoul.

CHAPTER EIGHT

FLOWERS from Raoul surrounded her with their fragrant mockery of love. A fresh bouquet every morning and this was Friday. If she saw him tonight, Ellen knew Raoul would overrule all her objections. She didn't love him. But Raoul's persistence was stronger than her denial. She must fulfill her decision never to be with him again. Otherwise, Raoul would own her on his own terms.

By six o'clock Ellen had lost all confidence in herself. She dreaded facing Raoul. Better to run like a coward than give in to him. In a way she was fighting for her life. Her moral life. She could see herself getting older and being cast from one man to the next until Warrie got old enough to realize what sort of person his mother was. She would rather die than have this happen.

The minutes ticked on. Ellen's tension grew. She went from room to room as though looking for a place to hide. Six thirty. In a burst of despair, Ellen flung on her coat and ran to the car. She turned on the motor and drove off without any idea of where she was going.

The car almost steered itself as her thoughts raced ratlike on a treadmill. In a frenzy of dazed confusion she parked outside of Nita's house. Ellen sat very still in the quiet car. Perhaps Nita would not be alone now. Richard might be in for supper. She felt in no condition for the social graces. But she could not drive around all night aimlessly. And if she went home in an hour or so, she faced the danger of Raoul coming back. Even Warrie would not be home until eleven.

Ellen had no choice but to take her chances that Nita would be alone. She patted her hair in a quick nervous gesture then hurried through the early night up to Nita's door.

A few moments later, Ellen stood looking up to Richard. She made no effort to appear casual but her eyelids were fluttering with anxiety and her breath came as though she had been running for blocks. Richard was a doctor. Ellen knew she could not fool him.

"I thought I'd take a chance and see if anybody was home," Ellen said.

"Well, I am," Richard said. "Does that help at all?"

"Very much." Ellen glanced at the pamphlet he was holding. "I'm not disturbing you?"

"Oh this?" he smiled. "A very poor second best to your company. Please come in. I need you to help me finish the beer Nita left."

Ellen came inside and took off her things, feeling less afraid now in the presence of his friendliness. As she settled herself in the living room, Ellen began to come out of her solitary nightmare. "Nita's out?"

"Just for awhile. She went in search of some tartar sauce, I think. We're having scallops and french fries at my request. I hope you haven't eaten yet." He straightened one cuff of his V-necked sweater and poured Ellen some beer. "I'm really driving the poor girl out of her mind," he said with amused apology.

We both are, Ellen thought. Yet she knew that Nita wasn't one to crumble easily. Nita seemed to thrive on helping others and Ellen thought it incongruous that she appeared to take such little interest in Joey.

"How are they treating you at the hospital?" Ellen could be interested in Richard's career because he didn't force it on her the way Jay used to.

"Pretty fine. I got a letter this morning from Washington. They're expecting me right after Christmas, if I decide to go."

"Will you?"

He set his glass on top of the pamphlet. "I don't know yet."

She wanted to make intelligent conversation about enzyme research, but she didn't know the first word about it.

"There are lots of reasons to keep me here," Richard said. "I could combine research at the hospital with a small private practice. Somehow, that seems righter than to be locked up in a laboratory all the time. Measles and chicken pox need attention too, I guess." He took off his glasses to wipe them and Ellen considered that his face looked young and old at the same time. The thoughtful eyes looked strained but not humorless. Age would not mar his appearance. Richard's experience would become an increasing display of compassion for all suffering creatures. By comparison Ellen's trouble seemed very small and unimportant.

Thinking back over the past couple of months, she realized the confinement of her own activities. Her life was bounded by the walls of her house and the short distances that she chose to drive. What had she seen or done or contributed to anybody's welfare? She hadn't even taken Warrie away for the summer vacation. As Richard talked, Ellen became inspired with all the fields open to her just for the asking. She could go to night school and take a course in psychology, maybe get a deeper understanding of the problems she couldn't handle by herself. Or maybe she would give some of her time as a nurse's aide at the hospital.

When Nita returned, Ellen's mood had changed from one of desperation to the new high spirits of self-worth.

"I understand it's fish dinner night?" Ellen said. She caught Nita's quizzical look and tried to convey her own sense of reassurance.

"Yes," Nita said. "Come peel potatoes."

"Bye bye, ladies," Richard said, leaning back against his chair like a monarch.

Ellen preferred for a man not to trespass into the kitchen. This added to her own sense of importance and gave her security in the knowledge that certain areas of living were her direct responsibility.

"Frankly, I'm surprised," Nita said. "But happily so."

Ellen opened the bag of potatoes. "I didn't care to face him," Ellen said. "If you'd ever met Raoul, I wouldn't have to explain."

"That's all right," Nita replied. She handed Ellen a peeler. "Running away is sometimes the first indication of sanity. I'm flattered that you came to me."

Ellen attended to the potatoes in silence as Nita opened a cardboard cylinder, poured out bread crumbs and mixed them with raw eggs and seasoning. She felt very content alone in the kitchen with Nita. She remembered years ago helping her mother roll dough for the bread she loved to bake. The thought sent a peaceful security to her being and she didn't question her happiness here with Nita. That Ellen should be a woman with a half grown child and still so much of a child herself did not occur to her now.

"Of course," Nita continued, "you won't be able to avoid Raoul forever. From what you tell me, he's not the kind to accept anybody's ultimatum. One of these days, you'll have to face him, Ellen. Alone."

"Let me not worry about that now. I want to enjoy the evening with you people and forget that Raoul exists."

"All right," Nita said. "But keep it in mind for later."

Nita went out to set the table and Ellen kept watch over the frying. She wished she didn't have to go home tonight at all. But it would be safe once Warrie was home. Raoul would have sense enough not to try to force her or make a scene in front of the boy.

At a quarter of eleven Ellen got ready to leave. Some of the misgiving began to assail her.

"Shall we ride home with you?" Nita said.

"You don't have to," Ellen replied in a voice not quite full of conviction.

"Look, Nita," Richard said. "You're expecting Joey any minute. Doesn't that give me a perfect excuse to take her home myself?"

Ellen agreed with enthusiasm. If, by any chance, Raoul did come by and saw her with another man, she wouldn't have to argue with him at all. Her "no" to Raoul would then be securely confirmed.

"Go ahead," Nita said. "But how are you going to get back here?"

"Ellen will lend me her car and you can return it in the morning."

Without waiting for further discussion, he got both their coats and took Ellen to her car.

Warrie came in almost directly behind them. He seemed very subdued from the evening's activities and made no attempt to conceal his yawns. That Dr. Wayne was at his home did not seem to surprise him. Nor, as Ellen noted, did he seem to object.

"I forgot to ask you the last time," Warrie said. "What do you call that thing again? The thing you put in your ears and listen to the heart beat?"

"A stethescope," Richard said. "Would you like to listen to one sometime?"

"Could I really?"

"Of course. You might decide to be a doctor yourself someday."

The thought was a long way off, but Richard's words secretly thrilled Ellen. She could think of nothing more wonderful than for Warrie to be a doctor. She believed that a physician was next to God. And she could afford to send Warrie to the best schools, if he wanted to study.

"That was very kind of you," she said to Richard after Warrie had gone off to bed.

"I'm just an old recruiter," he answered. "Think nothing of it."

But she understood that Richard wouldn't have bothered if he didn't consider Warrie to be above average in intelligence. He didn't try to take off his coat and force her hospitality.

"If you aren't busy tomorrow evening," Richard said, "maybe I can bring over the stethescope then?"

They were magic words which staved Raoul off for another night. "Come as early as you can," Ellen said.

"I'll do my best to get here by eight."

She had no choice but to accept this offer. Somehow she would manage to be out of the house until then and come back just in time for Richard to call for her.

Ellen arose very early the next morning. Raoul might drop by at any time. She had to hurry and get out of the house. Warrie was puttering around with breakfast and the smell of burning toast filled the house. Ellen went in to him.

He was examining a charred slice and scratching off some of the black with his fingernail.

"How on earth did you manage to do that with a pop-up toaster?" Ellen said.

"I don't know. It popped up the first time raw. And now it's burned. Maybe it's broken."

"You have to adjust the timer, dear. Here, look." Tactfully she helped him boil a couple of eggs and joined him in having a glass of orange juice and coffee.

"Is he really going to bring it over for me?" Warrie said, piling jam on a fresh piece of toast.

"Yes, I think so."

"He's nice. Do you think it's hard to become a doctor?"

Ellen refrained from allowing herself to take this conversation too seriously. "I think you should ask Dr. Wayne about that yourself, my dear. But I know it takes a lot of studying and good marks in order to get into medical school."

"That ends that," Warrie said. "I like Mr. Masters too."

She hadn't given much thought to Jay lately. He hadn't phoned or tried to get in touch with her. Perhaps he realized that there could be nothing more between them. He probably didn't take it too hard. He was so engrossed with his work that it couldn't make much difference to him. She thought it kind of Jay to allow their relationship to drift naturally apart.

Warrie brought one spoon and the dish to the sink. Then, considering his duties complete, went off for his hat and coat. "Look, Mom," he said standing at the door, "it's all right if you go out with anybody you want to." With that edict left for her consideration, he went out into the first flakes of snow.

Ellen went to the window and watched them drift lazily and melt into the earth. She thought of the cabin and the soggy drive to reach it. She didn't want to get stuck on the muddy mountain road. The weather was on her side if she should happen to run into Raoul. But if he came to the house now, she was alone. They would have enough privacy here not to need the cabin today. She phoned Nita and asked permission to come over again.

She couldn't impose herself on Nita indefinitely. There was a limit to how selfish she could be even in the interests of her own preservation. She was taking everything from Nita and giving so little in return. Somehow she must make it up to her. By the time Nita had come and picked her up, she had made up her mind. And the idea wasn't exactly distasteful.

Nita accepted Ellen's company with her usual non-committal approach. Ellen wished she knew what Nita was thinking behind her mask of nonchalance. She knew of only one sure way of discovering if Nita were contemptuous of her. For a moment Ellen watched Nita combing her hair before the bedroom mirror. Then she went over to the woman and kissed her on the back of the neck.

But Nita pushed her away gently. "You're fooling yourself, girl," she said with utter kindness.

Embarrassed, Ellen looked away.

"I want you to go back home, see Raoul and settle your situation with him once and for all. Then afterward … well … we'll see."

The truth of Nita's words stung. But she could not deny the truth. Life would become insane if she had to spend it running away from her own home all the time. Nothing was worth the price of living in fear. Without some little gesture of bravery she might as well give up. Even failure would be better than this dreading of it. Ellen needed tangible evidence of where she stood with herself.

"You're right," she said to Nita. "I'm sorry to inflict myself on you like this."

"Ellen, I hope you're making it sound worse than it really is. He's only a man, after all. They can't take too much punishment without seeking elsewhere for consolation. Let me know what happens."

So Ellen went back home and waited for Raoul.

All her life she had waited for somebody to do something for her or to her. When she had married Warren, she had felt as though the years before knowing him were a long wait for the ultimate culmination of their love. Then she had waited, cowlike, as Warrie grew inside her and came into the world. After Warren's death, she had waited for someone to drag her up from the morass of her own solitary darkness. Jay had tried. Raoul had taken over. Now Nita challenged her to accept the reins and do something definite to be responsible for herself. All right. She wouldn't sit and wait for Raoul now. She would phone him instead. Ask him to come over and have it out with him once and for all.

Sandy was not surprised to hear Ellen's voice on the phone. Without question, she put Raoul on to speak with her.

He said that he couldn't come over until after lunch and Ellen knew that he was just turning the knife a little bit more. She didn't care. The small triumph of having taken the initiative for once gave her an unsteady eagerness. Ellen rehearsed all the words she would say to him. How they had nothing in common except the vulgar plunging of their bodies.

She thought about taking a drink to bolster her nerve, then decided against it. Handling Raoul was something she wanted to do without artificial aids. Besides, alcohol might change her mind. There was no denying the temptation inside her not to give Raoul up after all. Bravely she had tried to stifle the voice of desire. Yet it would not go away simply because she wished it to. Had it been up to Ellen, she would not have been afflicted with this craving for love. If she were frigid or impotent, how happily she would live out the rest of her years in the occupation of helping Warrie to reach manhood.

As Ellen thought about triumphing over Raoul, she also wondered who would take his place. If Nita were the answer to her troubles, wouldn't she feel happier in the thought? Certainly she could not go back to Jay. She considered him and knew that her body was not pleased with the idea.

But she could not return to celibacy. To fool herself into believing this was possible would only add more complication to her predicament. And what of Richard Wayne? She dared not put any hope in him. If she permitted herself to become interested in him and he left for Washington, the frustration would finish her completely.

With every possible alternative denied her, Ellen thought that she should go away for awhile. A vacation would renew her. She would meet other people and perhaps find someone to accept her love. The sooner she realized and did something about her limited chances in this small town, the quicker she could find a solution to the plaguing desire for sexual partnership and the more exalting partnership of love.

Raoul took his time about coming over and it was almost three o'clock before he arrived.

"You're a strange woman, my sweet," he said, dusting the snow from his hat brim.

She saw that Raoul wasn't at all hostile and it made her suspicious. If he were the kind to throw off his feelings, she might begin to understand him a little better. But Raoul's motives were locked away someplace in the vault of his mind. Only Raoul knew the combination.

Ellen gave him a brandy and soda but took nothing for herself. She had to be very careful. She felt as though Raoul were circling around her looking for a point of attack.

"I asked you over," Ellen said, "because I wanted to settle our situation once and for all. There's no use in this cat and mouse game, Raoul. Neither of us is enjoying it."

"All right," he said. "Settle." But Raoul was too willing to listen, too agreeable.

As Ellen spoke, she felt her words lose conviction because he wasn't battling against them. After awhile the sentences petered out and she simply stood looking at him, waiting for his reaction.

"Do you expect me to disagree with you?" he said into the silence. They had reached the back terrace and Raoul looked out to the snow etching the hills with white tree tops. "You haven't said one word that isn't true. I know you don't love me. That point was proven quite sufficiently many years ago. And of course you have no reason to expect any other relationship to work over a long period of time. But don't you forget one thing?"

Ellen was afraid to ask what. She had managed to put herself at the furthest corner from him and stood behind a low wicker chair, grasping its frame so that the knuckles of her hands looked almost bare of covering.

"You don't have to hide, Ellen. I'm not going to jump you, after all. Unless that's what you want me to do." He put down his glass and started toward her. "I know you don't want me to touch you," he said. "So push me away."

Ellen stood very still. She wasn't going to run. How ridiculous for this man to chase her all over her own house. Instead she would prove to him just how much she didn't want him. If he took her in his arms, she would go limp, cold, and disinterested. Raoul didn't accept words. But he would believe lack of enthusiasm.

Rigidly Ellen waited, praying for the strength to carry out her plan.

"You might not care," Raoul said. "And it may be all wrong between us. But I need you, Ellen. Do you think I'd come chasing after you like this if you didn't mean anything to me?"

She didn't know what to think. Faithfully she must cling to her original decision. Raoul wasn't meant for her. No matter what sweet words he called to his aid, she mustn't listen to them.

"Darling Ellen," he whispered and kissed her tenderly on the forehead.

The touch of his lips shook her. There was no violence in his kiss. No sign of brutal passion. She had not expected him to approach her with such humanity.

"What can I do to prove myself to you?" he said. "I know I'm acting like a fool. It doesn't matter. I'd do anything, anything to keep you with me." His lips wandered down to her eyelids. She had never felt him so soft, so gentle.

Ellen said not a word. She hardly dared to breath. As he kissed her, she concentrated on not leaning the veriest inch toward him. But her lack of response did not deter Raoul. She felt his lips travel across her cheek and down to seek her mouth. Her lips parted and his tongue darted in to find her own. She twisted away from him. But he didn't try to force her back.

"You're the only woman I've ever wanted. Don't deny me, darling. Please don't shut me out after we've had so much together."

The urgency in his voice was so convincing. So convincing. The slow poison of Raoul's words began to take effect. Ellen felt the firmness of her decision beginning to thaw. She knew what it was to need someone. Even if there was no love to bless their union. In this world one had to be grateful for the shadow of love.

"Raoul, please," she said and her voice wavered. "You know I'll give in if you keep asking. But I don't want to. Can you believe that I would give my body to you and hate it while we are together?"

"I understand," he whispered. "And I don't ever expect you to forget Warren. Your nature is to be loyal. I admire you for it. But I know also that you can grow to be loyal to me. And I'm hoping for that, Ellen. You can't know how much I'm hoping."

What more could she say to him? His fingers cupped her chin and tilted her face like a flower to his own. Now, as their lips met, Ellen's body relaxed against his. He drew her slowly down onto the chair. Ellen stopped thinking. She knew only of the barrier of solitude which Raoul could push aside. He could trick her loneliness with the sleight of hand called sex. Her head went back and she felt his breath on her throat.

"Raoul, I hate us," she whispered. But the words were scattered by her desire.

Dizzily she became his plaything. His words, his hands, his body twisted her into a tautness of desire. Somehow they got to the bedroom.

Roughly he pulled off her clothes. She wanted him to be brutal this time and she knew that he sensed this longing in her. She fell down onto the bed, dragging him with her. He bit into her skin along the line of her heaving ribs and she cried out a soft note of pain. He ran his lips downward between her breasts and she burned as though he were spreading a trail of fire. She burned with misery and passion and uselessness. She grabbed him low on his back and pulled him on top of her.

She lifted herself, eager for his entry.

"Fast. Give it to me fast."

Her hips raced with incredible energy. The rounded flesh of her buttocks dimpled and tightened.

"Faster … faster." She seemed to be racing toward a distant and hopeless peak of satisfaction.

Well schooled in the by-roads of pleasure, Raoul kept the pace she desired.

Then, of a sudden, she wanted it slow and agonizing and not quite deep enough. She needed to torture herself for a while by pretending that she could not reach a climax. As she held herself at bay, her fingers dug into the chords of muscle on his shoulders, tense by her command to hold back.

She made him do many things which he had never done with her before. But this did not surprise him. He placed his mouth where she directed and she abandoned herself to a madness of sensation. There was nothing that could make her wilder than the feeling of Raoul's tongue.

Her mind floated someplace with the drifting snow as Raoul took her again and again. Without hope, without faith, without light, Ellen wandered in the pasture of her craving.

She lay on the bed when he had gone, between sleep and waking. A covering of hopelessness suffocated her wish to arise. Dimly she remembered that Richard would be calling for her soon. She didn't want to see him. She didn't want to face anyone. Without belief in herself, Ellen could not go among people and play the role of being a real person. She was not a person but a machine that responded inevitably and indiscriminately. What right had she to go among decent and civilized human beings?

Perhaps she should phone Dick and give him some excuse. He would not try to persuade her. She called the hospital and found that Dick had already left. She did not have the courage to phone Nita and admit what had happened. Nita had faith in her and Ellen had not lived up to that faith.

Yes, the best thing would be for her to go away for awhile. She must resurrect herself. If she remained here where Raoul had access to her, she would never get free. Her mind swung idly from thought to thought, without encouragement, without hope that she could be successful.

Ellen managed to sit up and made the attempt of pulling herself together so that she would be presentable when Dick arrived. The least she could do was not spoil his evening with her. For Dick's sake, she took a shower and polished her nails.

Supposing he saw through her facade? But he was too much of a gentleman to question her. She must make an effort to be good company. They would go dancing. Take dinner by candlelight at the country club. Ellen might introduce him to the couples they met. A young doctor should socialize.

The thought of doing good for somebody gave Ellen a little incentive. If she could find a crumb of herself that was not stale, she would be thankful. Dick wouldn't have to know anything about her. Let him believe that she was a carefree woman who had managed to resolve the difficulties of widowhood in a healthy and constructive manner. Oh, if only it could be true.

Ellen put on the orange dress because it added a touch of spirit. Though she didn't feel jolly, she must throw herself into the part and maybe it would come to her. With liquid make-up, she added color to her cheeks. The reflection of her face lied to her with youthful loveliness.

Richard arrived twenty minutes early with a white orchid. She hadn't expected that he really thought that they were going on a heavy date. But she could see the black bowtie between the upturned lapels of his coat. She allowed him to pin the corsage to her shoulder strap and leaned her head toward it, feeling that she might shame herself with tears any moment.

"If Warrie's home," he said, "I have the stethescope."

"I'm afraid he was discouraged when I told him what a lot of hard work it takes to become a doctor." She checked the things in her purse so she wouldn't have to look directly at Richard. Ellen knew she didn't have a poker face. She didn't want Richard to suspect the depth of her gratefulness for his sincerity. He might begin to think she liked him more than casually. Ellen didn't want him to get ideas. If he ever tried to make love to her, she would give in just as she had given in to Raoul. She wanted a chance to be decent with at least one person. And so far, her score was zero.

Ellen directed him to the country club and they took a table beside the glass wall. From that position they could look down to the forest of pine lighted by a string of colored bulbs for those who wanted to skate on the frozen lake.

"I'll have to make time for skating," Richard said. "That was the life, skiing home from school."

"In Europe?"

"Yes, Switzerland. Didn't Nita tell you? Her father was with the French consulate and my father was his underdog. We had a jolly time because I wouldn't give in about that."

"It must be beautiful in Switzerland this time of year. I'm thinking about taking a trip someplace. Where would you recommend?"

Her words took away Richard's smile for an instant but it returned almost immediately. "If you want cold dry air, Davos is wonderful."

"And for warm dry air?" Ellen smiled. She needed to make a joke of it. "I haven't really made up my mind whether it will be skiing or swimming or gambling."

"You can't lose with those choices. And what's going to make up your mind?"

"I suppose it will be impulse." The words had more truth in them than Richard knew.

The waiter brought roast chicken and small dishes of fresh vegetables so that their conversation was interrupted with the lighter subject of tasting and approving the wine.

Ellen kept looking about for people she knew in the hope that she could introduce Richard to them. The Trading Post set didn't come here. They had become bored with it years ago and preferred to patronize a shoddy bar half a mile down the road.

The so-called respectable element frequented this place with the continuing insistence of people who had squatters' rights.

And so Ellen was rather surprised to see Gloria and Michael Rancher come in accompanied by Gloria's parents. She supposed that Michael was already having fights with his new wife and considered this a great effort to make amends. She waited until Michael's group had seated themselves and ordered before she caught Gloria's attention. They nodded at each other and Gloria pointed out Ellen to Michael and her parents, who also nodded at Ellen with generously pleasant smiles. She saw them looking at Richard and asking each other if anybody knew him.

Ellen enjoyed the attention. She felt proud to be seen with Richard. He had no scandal attached to his name, he had a dignified and useful profession. And he looked like a human being one would like to know.

"Dance with me," she said, thinking to stop at Michael's table and show Richard off a little.

Ellen introduced him as Dr. Wayne and felt by their response that her evaluation of Richard was justified.

As the night went on, she had occasion to introduce him to others and Ellen knew that she was doing a good thing both for herself and for Dick. After Raoul today, she had no pride left to fuel her. Now, being with Dick, having the recognition of the people in the community who mattered, she felt a little bit more worthwhile. It might all be an illusion, but Ellen was grateful even for this semblance of dignity.

While Richard was driving her home, he said, "I didn't know you ran a social service."

Ellen was puzzled. Wasn't he glad to meet the very people who might comprise his professional practice?

"I thought you would appreciate a painless introduction to the wheels of this town," she said.

"Oh, I appreciate it all right, But I think you missed the point, Ellen. I took you out to be alone with you. My interest is in getting to know you, not assure myself votes for the next election."

"Well, I didn't plan the evening."

"Oh yes you did. You're deliberately trying to hide yourself from me. And I wish I knew why."

Ellen was trying to figure out why her intense conversations with people always took place in automobiles. Something about the intimacy of two people in a small space, unable to get away from each other, always trapped her. She meant well for Dick. He could appreciate her intentions even if he didn't agree with her manner of carrying them out.

"I'm sorry if I spoiled your fun," she said. She struggled with a helpless anger that could find no suitable outlet.

"Forget it," he said. "There'll be other times."

"No, I don't think so," she said. If she could deliberately cut Richard off now, it would save her a lot of trouble in the future. She wasn't up to his level. Their relationship was founded on deceit. He didn't suspect that she was having an affair with another man. He could hardly suspect that she had had an affair with the very woman whose house he lived in.

"You're a troubled girl, Ellen. I wish I could help. But there's no use in my trying to force you. Someday, I hope you'll square with me. It could mean a lot to us both."

They rode through the center of town and she saw the Christmas decorations already strung above the street. She thought of the families gathered around the tree, opening presents and exclaiming excitedly to each other. She could see the sparkle of tinsel decorating the dark green needles and the blue and red colored balls swinging from the limbs. Cranberry sauce and roast turkey surrounded by the parents and children united by the season's glow. No, she didn't want to spend Christmas here. She would take Warrie to a large city and cover their emptiness with hectic good times.

"I'm going away for awhile, Richard. If you're still here when I return, perhaps we can start our friendship over."

In her heart Ellen didn't want to count on this. Her experiences had proven too well that she couldn't have a normal relationship with anyone. She lived with an intensity that distorted her relationships and made them tools for lust. Sincerely she did not want this to happen between herself and Richard.

Ellen shook hands with him at the door, already thinking about how delicious it would be to get away from Raoul and her own weakness that was condemning her to a life of vulgarity.

The next day she went with Raoul to the cabin though she knew they would have difficulty reaching the place. Twice the tires caught in the mud and Raoul just barely managed to get them free. Ellen tried not to think what would happen if he were forced to go for help from the gas station in town. Raoul could leave for New York and not be hindered by the scandal which would smear them. But she would have to live with it and eventually face Warrie's accusations.

Yet all this was secondary to her thoughts of being with him. Her hatred and her needing intermingled, producing a flame of emotion that sought frantic gratification in Raoul's arms when they finally reached the cabin.

Each knew that this was the last time they could be together here and they drank deeply of the moments. She didn't tell Raoul of her planned vacation. She thought it would be better not to. He would have smooth words that might lure her to New York and she didn't want to take that chance.

They lay close and sapped the strength from each other's bodies. Ellen felt the bruises of Raoul's lips on her throat and touched them with disgust and self-contempt all the stronger because she had enjoyed receiving them.

"I'll send you train tickets for next Friday," Raoul said while they were dressing. "You can catch the four fifteen and I'll meet you in Grand Central at seven thirty."

There were two weeks before Warrie's vacation. She didn't really know whether or not she could resist getting on the train. Right now, she could tell herself no. But by next week, her body would not feel this deceiving strength of contentment. Oh, it was so easy to promise oneself the right thing when the body was satisfied.

"I'd rather not," Ellen said wearily. "It's not such a good idea to leave Warrie alone."

"Can't he stay with a friend?"

"We'll see."

Raoul didn't press her. He knew better than to try to make Ellen do something by force. His power lay in the seeming desire to acquiesce.

"Anyway," he said, "you'll have the tickets by Thursday. I know you'll make whatever arrangements are best."

She wished he would hit her, kill her, destroy her completely so there would be an end to this.

Yet the thought of Christmas vacation made it easier for Ellen to go to New York the following weekend. Because she promised herself the reward of never seeing Raoul again, she could glut herself now. The experience was like fulfilling a last wish on the death bed. Her weakness must be killed. Her sexual urges must be slayed by these last orgies. She listened to the wheels clacking along the rail and they were rushing like her heart beat to Raoul. Her greatest degradation was that she had given Warrie over into Nita's care for the weekend.

Nita hadn't said anything but she didn't need words to communicate her disappointment with Ellen. Ellen let herself dwell on all these thoughts, glad to hate herself as much as she possibly could.

New York was in a festive mood and didn't seem to care anything at all for Ellen's feelings. She rode with Raoul in a cab along Fifth Avenue and heard the carols being sung by voices coming from the large department stores. People gathered in front of the display windows, awed by the genius of automation that made stuffed animals skate and dance. On every corner a Santa Claus rang his bell, seemingly unaware of the slush and crowds that surrounded him. Rockefeller Center was packed with tourists taking photographs of the gigantic tree which towered behind the oval rink.

"I was afraid you wouldn't come," Raoul said as the taxi crawled with the rest of the traffic.

"Did you lose a night's sleep over it?" She couldn't help sharing her bitterness with him.

"Why don't you try to enjoy yourself for a change? You'll come home and take a bath. We'll have forty eight hours worth of wonderful moments. I'll try to make them wonderful for you."

Even her ears were revolted by these words. Yet there was no point in being anything but docile. She had come, after all. She had no reason to blame Raoul completely.

His apartment was much more simply decorated than Ellen had expected. Eight lavish rooms overlooked Central Park, but she didn't have to pick her way around the furniture to get to the windows. Swedish modern obviously chosen by Raoul contributed to the lack of clutter which lent a startling effect because of the vast floor spaces in between. Yes, only Raoul could have designed a room where two people had to sit on the same sofa in order to talk to each other comfortably.

A bottle of champagne stood in a silver ice bucket and he poured them each a drink. Ellen wanted to get drunk as quickly as possible so that she wouldn't have to remember where she was and what she was doing here.

They were too high up for any of the sounds of the city to reach them. Ellen felt locked away in a gorgeous dungeon with Raoul her jailer.

For two days she stayed with him. Raoul didn't seem inclined to take her out anywhere and Ellen didn't care if she never saw the light of day again.

She returned home exhausted and pale. The desire to sleep pressed heavily as she met Nita at the station.

"I thought it would be better not to bring Warrie along," she said. "So I dropped him off at the house first."

"Thank you," Ellen said. The two words embodied everything she felt toward Nita.

"Would you like to come freshen up a bit before we go home? Nobody's at my place. You can take your time."

"That would be a good idea," Ellen said. Somehow she thought that her appearance would scare Warrie, if she looked anything like she felt.

Nita ran a hot bath and discreetly refrained from asking any questions. "I didn't realize that Warrie was such a well behaved boy," she said. "He didn't give me any trouble at all and even offered to help with the dishes."

Ellen was thankful that Nita could touch upon the one bright spot in her life. "I won't ask this favor of you again, Nita." She let herself slide down into the hot water, wanting it to melt away the dirt from the crevices of her soul. "Next weekend I'll have enough strength to refrain, God willing, then I'm taking Warrie away for the holidays. He deserves a change and I certainly need one."

"That's the best thing you could tell me." Nita wiped the steam off the mirror and applied fresh lipstick. "Does Raoul know where you're going?"

"He doesn't even know I'm going." She held out her hand and Nita gave her a wash cloth. "I made arrangements to fly to San Francisco. Warren has relatives there. They'd like to see our son after all these years. It will do us both good to be with the family for Christmas." She sat up and let Nita soap her back. "If they're half as good to me as you are, I'll have a wonderful time."

"You'll have a wonderful time anyway. And so will I. Richard is going out of town also. I'm going to get a maid again and treat myself to the pleasures of being lazy."

"Try my Doreen. She's really dependable." As Ellen said these matter of fact words, she found herself thinking about Richard. She had acted wisely by not counting on him. What if she had allowed herself to believe something could grow and he picked himself up like this and left just as she had begun to trust him? But she was working too hard to convince herself that she didn't care. Actually she felt completely let down. Without admitting it to herself, she had hoped that with the New Year, she could start a new life. Richard had all the qualities she could depend upon with confidence.

"Will you leave the girl's number? I'll call the first thing in the morning." Nita tapped Ellen on the shoulder. "You weren't listening," she said.

"Yes I was. You said leave the girl's ..."

"I hope you're preoccupied with something pleasant for a change."

Ellen smiled a sorry grin that made her eyes large and bright. "I was thinking about Richard," she admitted now. "You probably will think I'm nuts but I thought there might be a chance with him. A new start, all that sore of foolishness."

"But I dragged out of him the fact that you didn't treat him very warmly the other night," Nita said. She put down the soap and Ellen rinsed herself by ducking down to her chin. Despite the abuse it had received, her body still looked young and vital, but Ellen was only dimly aware of this because she was listening attentively to Nita.

"I didn't treat *him* warmly," she said. "Nita, I did everything in my power to make that man feel at home." She gave the water an irritable slap.

Nita made no further comment. She gave Ellen a towel, then lay down on the bed and thoughtfully smoked a cigarette until Ellen had dressed herself. Then she took Ellen home and left her to greet Warrie.

Ellen approached the boy with a guilty trepidation. She didn't know how she would fare under the barrage of Warrie's questions. Better to talk about their coming trip to the West Coast.

"Did you have a good time?" he said to her with narrowed eyes. He was wearing a new pair of climbing boots that laced up to mid-calf and held a folding knife in a side pocket. Ellen wondered where he had gotten them.

"You know I missed you," Ellen said and it was true. "Those are pretty snappy boots," she said.

"Dr. Wayne got them for me," Warrie said, brightening for a moment. "And he let me try his stekascope."

"That's very nice of him." She was surprised that Richard had chosen to spend time with her boy. And she was ashamed for not having brought Warrie a present from New York. But she was never herself with Raoul. He managed to annihilate any small instinct of decency left to her.

"Have you decided where you want to sit in the plane?" she asked. This was going to be Warrie's first trip in the air. He should be very excited about it.

"The best place to sit is behind the wings so that they don't block your view."

She could tell that he was parroting this information. Had he discussed the trip with Richard? There's not going to be any snow in San Francisco, if you can imagine it," she said. "Won't that be strange, to spend Christmas in spring clothes?"

"I guess so. What did you do in New York?"

"But Warrie, I told you that before I left." She knew that children had an instinctive way of ferreting out liars.

"Tell me again." His hands had clenched into little fists and Ellen recalled this had been his old habit before Jay became interested in him. It frightened Ellen to see this retrogression.

"Now look, dear, there's no point in going over all that again. I'm very tired. New York was crowded and it wasn't much fun, believe me. I'd love to have a cup of tea with you and go to sleep."

He didn't want any tea and he didn't want any evasions. She could feel his distrust and it made Ellen miserable. She couldn't take the risk of losing Warrie's confidence. If she lied, he would know. She certainly couldn't tell him anything close to the truth. How she hated Raoul. How she hated herself. If emotions could cause so much damage to people, she wondered why they were born with them.

And through all this, she wanted to know what had prompted Richard to buy Warrie the boots. Did he feel sorry for the child or recognize what Ellen was doing in New York? Certainly Nita wouldn't tell him. Her confusion was a paralyzing force and she wished Warrie would go to bed and leave her alone with herself. Why couldn't he look forward to San Francisco? She was trusting that the change would work miracles for her. Ellen had nowhere else to put her faith. If she didn't recuperate out West with the family, there would be no hope for her.

"I'm going to bed," Warrie said with a tight jaw that begrudged the words. "But I still think you had a good time in New York."

He left her alone and Ellen went to make herself a cup of tea. She had hardly eaten anything during the weekend and her stomach felt like an open wound.

She mustn't think about herself. Certainly she had no right to feel sorry for her condition. Tomorrow she must go out and buy Christmas presents for the family. If she had been in her right mind, she would have picked them up in New York. She sat down with the tea and made a list of all the people to be included. Warrie's grandmother, her sister-in-law Stephanie who had never gotten married and still lived at home. Assorted nieces and nephews to whom she would mail packages. These were all on Warren's side since her own family had dispersed when her mother died. Of course she must get something special for Nita. Would it be proper, she wondered, to pick up some little thing for Richard since he had been so generous with Warrie? She would look and see. Cards to Jay and the Vernes in general. And a new purse for Doreen.

Ellen finished her tea and went to bed trying to forget her trip to the city. But it seared her mind and she dreamed the incident all over again. The next day, she forced herself to attend to the shopping. For Nita, she found a book of Japanese poems which said so gracefully all the beautiful thoughts Ellen cherished for the woman.

The problem of Richard was a little more difficult. She didn't know very much about his personal tastes and to buy something wearable was too intimate. As a last resort, she went to the medical supply outlet and found a black visiting case of Italian morocco. She thought at first that so expensive a present would be out of order. But she bought it anyway. From it he would know that she was aware of his attention to Warrie, which was the most priceless gift that anyone could give to her.

Shopping completed, Ellen returned home and started to wrap. It was a harmless occupation to keep her from brooding. Christmas was still twelve days off. What would she do with herself tomorrow and the day after that?

But Nita began to take up more of her time. She invited herself over and took Ellen out to lunch. They went to a play which had just opened for the season. One night they drove beyond the hospital and dined at a Mexican restaurant which Ellen had never been to before. At no time did Nita mention anything about their night together. They acted like two ordinary friends who enjoyed each other's company without other implication. Ellen accepted

Nita warmheartedly, especially since she was always so full of information about Richard. She didn't pump Nita. She had no need to do so since Nita was so generous with her anecdotes. As the days went by, she began to know Richard with an insight she would never have been able to manage without the benefit of Nita's assistance.

All of what Ellen learned pleased her. Richard played chess and Richard liked Dixieland jazz. In college he had played the drums and won notoriety for being the nosiest sophomore of the year. Ellen found this hard to believe and yet it was consistent with his appetite for life. No good doctor, she thought, could function with highest success unless he almost worshipped the sweet things that life could give. This worship made of death an even keener enemy to be battled.

When the weekend approached, Nita invited Ellen over to spend it at her place. Ellen realized why Nita did this. She accepted the offer with honest thankfulness.

She tore the train tickets which arrived in the mail and burned them. A wave of relief swept over her as she watched the flakes of charred paper drop into the sink. Maybe she was through with Raoul. At least she was on her way to being through with him. One thing she owed herself was not to permit her thoughts to wander in his direction. Every time his face came into her mind, she would lift a mental hand and push it away. Why should she care if he waited at the station for her?

Nita had invited several people over to the house for bridge. She had played occasionally but wasn't very good at it. Richard didn't play either. Nita set up a table for the others and got out an old chess set for Richard.

"Why don't you teach Ellen," she said. "It's such a fascinating game," her voice was filled with amusement.

"Let's talk instead," Richard said.

"No, I'd like to learn, if you're game to teach me." She didn't really care about chess but she wanted to void getting too friendly with Richard. He was leaving soon. She didn't want to upset herself with thoughts of anything more than frivolous between them.

The people at the bridge table were couples Ellen had seen at the benefit performance. They were mostly older than herself and rather serious about getting on with the bridge. She didn't feel rude by not prolonging conversation with them. They didn't seem Nita's kind of people either, but she saw that Nita was right at home serving snacks and sitting in when the time came for her turn at the table.

"Now this whole row of fellows is called pawns," Richard began. "They can move like this or like this, or like this to capture an opposing piece."

Immediately Ellen could see that the game was too complicated for her comprehension. Nor did she have the peace of mind to concentrate on it. She peeked up at Richard and saw that he was peeking down at her. They both laughed.

"Shhhhh," he cautioned. "We'll disturb the bridge players."

People who were devoted to chess were supposed to be stuffy and look down on those who couldn't or didn't want to be bothered. But Richard was taking her incapacity with good humor. Ellen thought of him driving everyone crazy with his drums. He would never be a stodgy old goat.

As the evening proceeded, Ellen felt a comfortable part of the gathering. True, she exchanged only an occasional word with someone other then Richard, but everybody accepted her because she was Nita's friend. She could imagine having gatherings like this at her own place where people could spend an evening of enjoyment without needing to be noisy or frantic. This was a good way to live, she thought. Then Ellen realized that part of the goodness was Richard's company.

CHAPTER NINE

ELLEN decided that instead of giving Richard his gift, she would
have it delivered by Nita just before she got on the plane. That
way, she wouldn't have to face him and go through the discomfort
of saying good-byes. Thank heaven, she hadn't allowed Richard
to become very important to her. As the days went along, Warrie
became more and more enthusiastic about their impending trip.
He had, apparently, either forgotten or forgiven her disappearance to New York. She hardly realized how little importance
Warrie placed on the matter until late one afternoon when she
had returned from town after a sojourn with Nita.

"You had a phone call," Warrie said. "Long distance."

"Oh?" Ellen became immediately alert. She didn't care about
Raoul's disappointment in not finding her at home. But she was
very concerned about what Warrie thought of it.

And Warrie was very nonchalant. "I never spoke to anyone
so far away. It sounded like he was right around the corner." He
squatted before the cleaning closet and came up with a container
of saddle soap. Then he took off the boots and began to polish
them. "They're peachy boots, Mom, don't you think?"

She waited until Warrie had wet the sponge and seated
himself cross-legged on the floor. "What was the conversation
about?" Ellen said, attempting to be just as nonchalant.

"Nothing. We just went into the store and I told the man my
size."

"I mean on the telephone." She kept her voice very sweet and
tried not to let her anxiety show.

"Oh that. Well, he told me who he was and I told him who I was. Then he asked if you would be home soon and I said I didn't know because we were getting ready to go away. And he asked where. And I said San Francisco. And he asked when we would be back. And I told him. Then he asked me to write down his telephone number in case you wanted to call him back. I put it under the phone."

A wave of nausea began in Ellen's stomach. She couldn't admonish Warrie. He had boasted innocently of the trip which was exciting to him. It was only natural that he should be willing to give any information asked for.

Well, there was nothing Raoul could do to prevent her from going. Maybe the information also told him how much Ellen didn't want to keep their relationship alive. But, of course, he already knew that Ellen was not a truly willing partner in their affair. This was not important to Raoul. His satisfaction was this very unwillingness: that Ellen must go to him despite herself. When would this come to an end for her? How could she tear herself free from the most loathsome yet most necessary thing in her life?

Ellen went to the telephone and ripped into shreds the piece of paper with Raoul's number.

Ellen concentrated her attention on gathering Warrie's wardrobe and her own for the trip. She bought flight weight luggage and promised Warrie that they would get California stickers to paste on.

The day before her departure, Ellen invited Nita out to lunch. They went to a gypsy tea room at an obscure corner of town, knowing they would be relatively alone.

Neither paid much attention to the food. Ellen felt that she was going away forever instead of just ten days.

"What are we so sad about?" Nita laughed. She reached into her purse and withdrew a tiny box wrapped in tissue paper. "Put this under the tree for yourself."

Ellen held the present delicately. She wanted to open the beautiful package now. But at the same time, she was glad that she would be alone when the time came. Ellen wasn't so sure that she might not yield to tears and she didn't want to inflict her silly emotionalism on Nita.

She set the box carefully into her own bag. "Will you take us to the airport?"

Nita studied the tea leaves settled at the bottom of her cup. "I've already planned to do so," she said softly.

Ellen's presents for Nita and Richard were in the back seat of her car. When she dropped Nita at home, Ellen gave them to her. "Don't tell Richard until after I've left," she said. "I don't want to embarrass him."

"All right," Nita smiled. "But nothing embarrasses Dick."

As Ellen packed the last small items into the valises that night, she felt the afternoon's sadness growing inside her. But Warrie was making a nuisance of himself, trying to jam in his catcher's mitt and other beloved possessions, which saved Ellen from becoming altogether depressed.

Ten o'clock the next morning, she answered Nita's ring. Richard stood behind her, hunching his head so that the falling snow would not spot his glasses. The sky was a pure white unruffled by the wind.

"I'm good for carrying baggage," Richard said. He stepped inside and hefted the waiting valises, but he did not neglect to use Warrie's help too. Richard gave Warrie the keys. "You want to go ahead and open the trunk?"

"You bet," Warrie said and he ran out, tracking oversize footsteps in the carpet of snow.

Ellen was overwhelmed by the little party which had come to see her off. Nita hadn't mentioned that Richard was going to join her. She felt almost honored by his effort. She knew that he must have taken time away from the hospital to come along.

"All the windows locked?" Nita said as Ellen took a final survey of the house. "Leave a note for the milkman?"

"Stop making jokes," Ellen said.

From the front seat of the car Warrie called, "Let's go!"

With a final sigh, Ellen turned the key in the front door lock. The air smelled dry and almost warm as she hastened with Nita to the car.

Both women got into the back seat. They chatted about domestic details as Warrie listened to Richard telling him about dragsters.

They reached the airport in plenty of time and Richard checked the luggage through. He came back and gave Ellen the tickets. His systematic method of accomplishing incidentals relieved Ellen of some of the nervousness that possessed her. But she could not manage to rid herself of the clinging sadness which had begun the other day.

The drawling voice came over the loud speaker and people began moving up to form a line near the gate.

"Have a good trip," Nita said and kissed Ellen on the cheek.

Ellen shook hands with Richard and thanked him for helping.

"Take care of your mother," he said, shaking hands with Warrie. "And bring her back safely."

Ellen and Warrie walked out onto the airfield and climbed the high metal steps onto the plane. They found seats behind the wing and Ellen looked out the window to see the tiny figures in the distance. Now she knew where the sadness came from. As they fastened their seatbelts and the plane began to rumble down the runway, Ellen realized she would probably never see Richard again.

Warrie's barrage of questions kept Ellen from permitting herself to think about this too much. She had to try to explain about the propellers, though she didn't really know why an airplane stayed in the air. The stewardess came and gave them some chicklets and Warrie found post cards in the pocket attached to the seat in front of them. Then he noticed the air vent above the window and insisted on turning the switch.

When the plane finally landed, Warrie was completely subdued. Warren's sister Stephanie met them and greeted Ellen with a maternal hug deflected from her own lack of husband and children. Her graying red hair frizzed out from the bun on her thin neck and she wore a flowered print dress which displayed pale freckles above her flat chest.

"My, you're a big fellow," she said, bending down to kiss Warrie. "He looks the very image of his father, doesn't he, Ellen?"

Stephanie's awkward attempts soured Warrie almost immediately. "I look like myself," he said.

"But I think you have your mother's nose," Stephanie bubbled on, unaware of her effect upon Warrie. "Did you have a good trip? I'm sure you must be starving. We have a nice hot dinner waiting. Mother was so anxious. She wanted to come along too. But she wheezes so. I hate to take her out in the station wagon. It's so drafty. And this fog. I'm sure you never saw such a fog. We love it, you know. I think it has mystery and dignity like a ..." Stephanie's imagination failed before the grandeur of her unexplored soul.

A porter flung the baggage into the back of the old Ford and Ellen tipped him.

"We can all three sit in front," Stephanie twittered. "I want both of you to have the full effect of our magnificent San Francisco hills."

Ellen could see that Warrie's patience was beginning to ebb rapidly as he sat squeezed in between the two women. Instead of looking out the window, he peered down at Stephanie's narrow feet working the clutch and the brake.

"You can see Coit Tower just ... around ... this ... corner. There."

Ellen looked at the tall cylindrical building but Warrie didn't bother. She was grateful that he was tired out. The chances of him saying something too out of place were smaller.

Stephanie drove the wagon energetically up and down the winding streets with a continuous chatter as though she were accustomed to speaking to herself. They reached an old brown-stone house of three stories. "Good," Stephanie said. "My parking space is still free."

Ellen looked at the white shades pulled exactly one third of the way down on each window and wondered if it was going to be too terribly dark inside. Perhaps some of Warrie's cousins had already arrived. That would help matters considerably. Warrie took one of the valises and dragged it up the stairs as Stephanie took the other, protesting that he was too little for such a heavy bag.

They went into the heavily carpeted and fringed parlor. Ellen saw Warrie's face brighten for the first time as the pungent odor of Virginia ham came to his nostrils.

"Mother," Shephanie called. "We're here."

Ellen sat down on a green plush sofa and fidgeted with her gloves as Warrie picked up and put down the porcelain figurines of Siamese cats and deer and chipmunks which cluttered every available shelf or table.

An old woman strode into the room who had Stephanie's highboned features, but held together with the foundations of an authoritative personality. She stood forcibly erect, painfully, Ellen thought. No doubt she was making an effort not to allow her clogged lungs to interfere with her greeting.

She took Ellen's hand and squeezed it with cold fingers and kissed her on the cheek with wrinkled lips. Then she turned to Warrie.

"You remember your grandmother," Ellen said.

"Why should he," Mrs. Tendler said. "We haven't seen each other since he was two and a half. Would you like to shake hands with a grumpy old lady?" she said to Warrie.

"Oh mother," Stephanie said. "You depress me with that kind of talk."

"Then go set dinner so you won't have to listen," the old lady snapped.

Warrie put down a tiny elephant and looked at her with the beginnings of a smile. "You're funny," he said.

"That's a good beginning for any friendship," she replied. "Wash up so we don't have to wait for you at the table."

"Okay."

Ellen felt the delicate balance shift in favor of a rewarding vacation. She could relax and enjoy herself with these people who were so anxious to make her feel at home.

They went in for dinner and Warrie set to with unabashed verve. Stephanie receded into the background and looked as faded as the wall paper. What did she dream of these many years, alone in her virginal bed, listening to the sounds of couples strolling under the haze of the moon? How did she accept the change of seasons year after year, knowing that the flower of her own youth had long ceased to blossom? But if she had never known a man's kiss, perhaps she could not really know what she had missed. Secretly, Ellen hoped that Stephanie had once taken a lover. Even were it just for one night.

Ellen slept in the musty house feeling safe because Raoul was so many miles away. During these ten days, perhaps she could learn to imitate Mother Tendler's control.

The old lady sat in her chair and directed the decoration of the Christmas tree. Stephanie brought out a ladder and climbed it, leaning out to the uppermost limb and looking very much like a praying mantis as she set the star in place. Warrie piled the presents around the base. Mrs. Tendler insisted that he help because she did not believe that he believed in Santa Claus.

"Of course I don't," Warrie insisted. And because she argued so furiously with him, Ellen saw that Warrie was almost converted by his own rebuttals to the contrary.

Christmas Day the rest of the family arrived from Berkely. The sound of children spinning the wheels of their new roller skates and playing King Arthur with Grandmother's new cane for a sword gave Ellen a warmth and contentment she had not known for many a year.

Ellen managed to go off by herself to open Nita's present. She flipped up the lid of the box and saw a single pearl raised in a narrow setting of gold. The solitary elegance was everything that meant Nita. Through blurred vision, Ellen slipped the pearl on the ring finger of her right hand. She wondered what destiny had in store for this magnificent person who must have tried with untold agonies to fit herself into a world that would not accept her. Ellen knew that if she accomplished nothing else, she must not take advantage of Nita's sympathies. They would have a sincere and solid friendship. But for Nita's sake, it must never again go beyond the bounds of what Ellen could honestly give.

For three days Ellen kept up a visiting spirit. Mother Tendler insisted on going with them to Fisherman's Wharf and showed Warrie how to bait the crab cages. Ellen would have managed to continue her disguise as a happy mother for the duration of their stay if she had been allowed to. Though at night her body reached out in dream's of a man's caress, she could sweep this away with the daylight.

Warrie was out with his skates one day and Stephanie had gone to the knitting store for yarn to finish the sweater she had started for him. Mother Tendler insisted that Ellen put polish on her ridged nails.

As Ellen stroked the ether-smelling liquid, Mother Tendler said, "Isn't it about time you got married again?"

The brush almost went up on the old lady's cuticle.

"Let's not fool each other," the woman continued. "You're not like my Stephanie, thank God. You're young and healthy and I think you need a man. Isn't that so?"

How could she talk with Warren's mother about something like this? "Warrie takes up so much of my time," she said.

"Of course. But not all of it. I would be very happy to see you married again. Work on it, Ellen. Don't get into the habit of living alone."

Never again did Mother Tendler bring up the subject for discussion. She had made her point and there was no use in repetition.

The woman's advice came to Ellen at odd times during the week. She put her face into the pillow and tried to smother the desperation that encircled her. Her body had begun to crave once more. She tried not to think of Raoul but the memory of his passion surrounded her. Only distance kept her secure from him. She didn't want to go back East, ever. Here, she could lie alone and know that her yearning must remain unfulfilled. But once back home, he would start with her again. Already she could feel the pull of his promised satisfaction to her body.

Stephanie drove them to the airport and waved a generous sized handkerchief as the plane rose into the air.

"Did you have a good time?" Ellen said when they were safely aloft.

"Sure did. I wish it could last longer even if Aunt Stephanie is a drip."

Ellen wished it could have lasted longer too. She looked forward without confidence to their return. She had wired Nita confirming their arrival. Nita would do everything in her power to help Ellen refrain from seeing Raoul. But in the last analysis, nobody could really help her but herself.

The plane circled and landed, returning them to the wintery blasts that swept sleet and snow like whiplashes. Ellen and Warrie ran toward the warmth of the waiting room and came almost directly into Raoul's arms.

Ellen stopped abruptly. He was all smiles and generous concerns as though they had parted the best of friends. Anxiously looked beyond him for Nita but she could not find the safety of her presence.

"Welcome home," Raoul said. "How are you, Warren? You know who I am. We talked on the phone long distance. Remember?"

"Sure I remember. You're Raoul Verne."

Ellen stood helpless as she listened to her boy engaged in seemingly innocent conversation. She had no excuse to take him away. Where, oh where was Nita?

"You're looking well, Ellen." Raoul reached out and took both her hands. She felt him press an envelope into her palm. Automatically her fingers closed around it. She slipped the envelope into her pocket. Why didn't she drop it into the nearest waste can and show Raoul her true lack of interest? But just the sight of him in his dark gray coat recalled the other picture of him, lying with her, stimulating the tortured desires and giving them surcease.

"I'll collect your baggage and we'll drive back to the house."

"No," Ellen said with a brave show of firmness. "I'm expecting somebody."

Raoul chuckled without comment.

Ellen's eyes remained on the door. Then, wonder of wonders, a tall figure with thick glasses came striding into the waiting room.

"Hi there" Richard said. "I'm surprised the plane wasn't delayed. You should see the road. Piled every inch of the way." Warrie slapped him on the elbow and shook his hand energetically. "How's the stethescope boy?"

"Wait till you see the things I got," Warrie said.

Ellen succumbed to a muddle of confusion and joy and relief that left her speechless. At last she said, "Dr. Wayne, this is Raoul Verne, an old friend from New York."

She watched the two men greet each other and for the first time noticed Raoul appear uncertain.

"Dr. Wayne," he said formally and extended his hand in conventional greeting.

"If you need a lift," Dick said, "we'll do the best we can for you."

"No thanks. I have my own car."

"Well, glad to know you. Let's go, Warrie."

Ellen went ahead of them as Dick and Warrie each managed a suitcase. Dick could hardly realize what he had done to help her.

"How about a welcome home dinner," Richard said. "If you're not too pooped."

"I'm not," Warrie said.

"This is between your mother and myself," Dick replied.

"Why?" Warrie asked.

"Face it, boy. You're a man and she's a woman." Richard caught Ellen's reflection in the rear view mirror and winked.

"Phooey."

Ellen's hand went surreptitiously into the pocket of her coat. She wondered what Raoul had given her. Her fingers traced the metallic outline of a key. So he had expected she would return panting after him. A sneer made her face ugly. How right he was, damn him.

"I thought you would be in Washington by now," Ellen said.

"So did I," Dick replied. "But I decided to stay with the hospital. There's a lot to accomplish here."

"For how long?"

"Permanently."

She couldn't dare to hope that Richard might have intentions about her. Other consideration had decided him.

"Well, how about that dinner?" Dick persisted.

"Yes, I'd love it." Ellen didn't know why she was accepting. Perhaps to keep that barrier between herself and Raoul. Perhaps she was grateful to him for having saved her at the airport. Perhaps because Warrie enjoyed his company.

He dropped her at the house and promised to return at six thirty. Ellen didn't bother to unpack. She went to take a hot shower and make herself as alluring as possible. The tiredness which had possessed her limbs during the flight was gone now. She felt only that old, too familiar stirring in her thighs. The thirst for sex was a need which no sleep, no ease could stop. The key lay untouched in its envelope, daring her to throw it away. Supposing that Richard made a plaything of her as Jay had? She did not have the strength for decorum or nonchalance. Or perhaps Richard was thinking it would be nice for them to go to bed. She must not allow this. So far, she managed to portray the decent woman with him. If Richard took her and discovered the eagerness with which she gave herself, she would lose his respect. And respect was hard to come by.

The only way she could hold Richard off would be by having Raoul on the side. Tormented by this ugly knowledge, Ellen continued to dress herself with unhappiness dispelling the pleasure of her attractive image.

Sharply at half past six, Richard returned. Warrie answered the door and Ellen heard them talking about the old army helmet which Mother Tendler had given to Warrie.

She put on the last touches of fragrance, added a smile to her unwilling lips and came out to greet Richard.

"Nita sends you her love," Richard said with a tender quality unabashed by Warrie's presence.

"Love, love, love," Warrie said with disdain. "Go on out and have your party. I don't care."

Richard helped Ellen into her coat. The key in her pocket seemed to weigh heavily.

"Where are we going?" she asked brightly.

"Wherever you like. I reserved tables at Ruggio's, The Mill and the country club. Madame's choice."

Richard treated her with such infinite respect. She must be careful to preserve this allusion for him. "Ruggio's will be nice again. I liked the orchestra."

They got into the car and Ellen waited for what he would say next. She didn't want to push or steer him toward any words which he did not intend to say of his own volition. But Richard didn't seem to be inclined to say anything either.

Ellen felt that she had to break the silence. "I'm glad you're not in Washington," she offered.

"So am I. This town has something Washington could never offer me." They were going so slowly that Richard didn't have to keep his glance fixed on the road.

"What's that?"

"You."

Ellen felt a thrill of happiness. But she must not let it run away with her.

"You see, I thought about the possibilities out there, the research lab, the opportunities. I even went so far as to write a letter of acceptance. But then I thought about you and tore it up." He smiled at her with a gentle consideration. "I trust that I haven't made a wrong prognosis."

But he wasn't saying anything that Raoul had never said too.

"Tell me more," she said breathlessly. Ellen could imagine him with his glasses off, nuzzling his long serious face between her breasts. But she could not accept Dick without the sanctity of marriage. She had no intention of spreading her disgrace further than the areas of Raoul and Nita. Dick must be kept safe from her passion. She refused to tie herself to him in an illicit relationship that would burden him and ruin his reputation in a town where he was just getting started.

"All right, I'll tell you everything," Dick said. "I had a number of long talks with myself. They all added up to only one conclusion. Ellen I love you."

Was that all that he wanted to say to her? Perhaps for a woman without Ellen's guilt this would be sufficient. But she wanted to hear words that would secure her future. She needed to hear all the precious promises that would quench her desire for Raoul.

"Could we be happy together?" Ellen said. "I have a child and a home already established."

Richard patted her hand with confidence. "If we could pull off this road," he said, "I'd show you how happy we could be together." Then he leaned across and touched her lips with his. It was a brief kiss but Ellen felt her body flare up.

"Warrie and I get along together," he continued. "I'm sure he'll accept me. Not as a second father, of course. But as a pal."

Ellen knew this was true. She had watched them closely. Warrie was interested in Dick for many reasons. Dick inspired him to think about his future. Vaguely Warrie was beginning to realize there was more to life than baseball games. Dick could help him mature into a man Ellen would be proud of. And Dick could help Ellen too.

"Darling," he said, "I would be the happiest man alive if you would marry me."

Ellen's breath caught in fantastic delight and her heart pounded almost out of her chest. "My dearest Richard," she whispered. "Of course I'll marry you."

She could not thrust her body upon him. The moving automobile required all of his attention. Then they were in the restaurant and all she could do was return the pressure of his hand. On the dance floor she moved very close to him, but social decency forbade that she make a show of her desire. There would be time after he took her home. Alone in the living room, they could display their love and she need never fear Raoul again.

Ellen managed to curb herself until they were in the privacy of her home. She switched on the smallest lamplight to preserve the intimacy that she needed to share with Dick.

"Come to me," she breathed, closing her eyes and holding out her arms for his embrace.

The room still had the musty odor of closed windows but Ellen did not care. She waited, expecting Richard, and he pressed her in his arms. Ellen could not accept his kiss alone. The weeks of solitude had dissolved her resistance. She clung to Richard and thrust herself tightly against him, unable to let go, needing him to search out her desire and sate it with his sure knowledge.

"We can be married right away," he whispered. "No long engagements."

But his hands failed to seek out the hidden resources of her need. His kisses remained proper symbols of love. The greedy senses which ruled Ellen failed to drag Richard into their clawing labyrinth. Her hands wandered over his body and he took them, holding her fingers at rest between his own warm palms.

Of course he was right, Ellen thought. To snatch at love hastily like dying victims of a disease was beneath Richard and his evaluation of her. She could not press him into intercourse for its own sake. Love, for Richard, was more than sex. And it was more than sex for Ellen too. But she did not have the stability to keep the promise in reserve for the night of their marriage. Little did Richard suspect the torments which tore at Ellen.

"I'd better go now," he said.

Unwillingly Ellen allowed him to take his leave. At the door, he kissed her good-night, then he was gone.

She stood alone with her desire alive and screaming in the core of her body. But she must fight it with every ounce and remnant of good sense and control. First of all, she had to get rid of the key. She must not leave it in the reach of temptation. Ellen went to the closet and found the envelope. A piece of paper was folded around the key. No, she wouldn't read it. But irresistibly her eyes flicked over the address printed in Raoul's handwriting. Why, it was the new motel just ten minutes out of town. He was waiting there for her now. She flung the key into the garbage pail and ran to the bedroom.

The night gave Ellen no rest. She paced the room and tried to blot out the image of Raoul lying on the bed, patiently waiting for her. Of course she wouldn't go to him. The thought was preposterous. She must imagine only Dick and the life they could have together. Ellen got out a bottle of Scotch and took a heavy dose, praying that it would release her from the torment eating through her body. Then she went into the bathroom and stood in the needle spray of the ice cold shower. But her skin was numb to everything except the flaring torch that seared throughout the length of her being.

The telephone rang through the darkness. Ellen hastened to the receiver, yearning for Richard's voice to soothe her.

But Richard's voice did not say hello. She slammed the receiver into the cradle, not wanting to allow herself one syllable from Raoul. Again the phone rang. Ellen disconnected them once more, then she left the receiver off the hook. In the black silence, she heard the operator clicking to see if anything was wrong.

"Go away," she sobbed into her pillow. "Leave me alone."

But neither sleep nor Richard nor the happiness soon to be hers gave her respite. Enervated with torment and the ceaseless pounding of her nerves, Ellen waited out the night.

Eight o'clock came and she phoned Richard at the hospital. But he couldn't spend the day with her. How could Ellen say that she needed him more than the laboratory, that her sickness was greater than any child's pain? He would rush to her tonight at six.

Ten long hours. Ten dreary and savage hours to pound at her and wear away the last strength she had for fighting. Ellen saw Warrie off to school and flung herself on the couch in the living room.

When Raoul came in, she did not move or say one word. He had only to take her.

The days went by and Richard suspected nothing of Ellen's double life. She presented to him a smiling, contented person, though her heart was ravaged with fears and guilt. They talked about living quarters and decided that it would be best to buy another house. A fresh start for them both. Ellen smiled bitterly to herself at the idea. She could not foresee a future without the spoilage of Raoul. He could continue to have her even beyond marriage. The threat of blackmail loomed over Ellen with its gloom and disaster.

By now Warrie knew that his mother was engaged to be married. The idea had settled well with him. He looked forward to many things with Richard, visiting the laboratory and learning more about the instruments that Dick carried in the bag Ellen had given him for Christmas.

"If you're going to marry Richard," Warrie said to her one day, "why do you still see the other guy? I thought it was against the rules."

Ellen's thoughts skidded to a halt. She didn't know how Warrie had discovered her deceit, but it was enough that he knew. Perhaps he had already mentioned this to Richard. How sickening for Richard to hear such words spoken in all innocence from the lips of a child. Ellen cast about in her mind for a solution. But she knew that her love for Richard would force her to tell the truth.

She could not manage to tell him that night. Nor did she have the courage to reveal her troubled thoughts on the night after that. All lay hopeless and dead in her heart. Decency demanded that she break the engagement. No matter what Richard thought of her, she could not allow him marriage to a person like herself. He deserved a decent woman.

Perversely the utter desolation in Ellen's heart gave her strength to repel Raoul. Her desire for sex was distorted into such a miserable burden of guilt that it no longer gave her pleasure. Day after day she locked the door. Raoul on the other side of it stood persistently ringing the bell but she would not go to open her house to him. The phone rang almost every fifteen minutes. She felt that Raoul was being impelled by a cold fury. He bombarded her with calls and telegrams and more calls. Ellen hid herself from him. She was beginning to take a weird delight in denying the claims which sex thought it had a right to make on her.

For two weeks she managed not to see Raoul at all. And from this abstention grew the strength to reveal the foul truth of herself to Dick. For his sake, for the sake of her son, Ellen knew that she must absolve the burden in her heart through confession. Only God alone would know the price of her repentance.

To make her revelation proved even more difficult than Ellen had expected because Richard was in a festive mood that Sunday afternoon. February had frozen the world around them into an icy bleakness, but the roads were cleared enough for driving.

"I've found it," Richard said, swinging her into his arms and planting a large kiss on her lips. "Come let me show you. The most wonderful house you've even seen. It even has a special wing for an office."

Dully Ellen permitted him to take her out to the rambling house of fieldstone. She had not known that the place was for sale. It stood in a protection of valley and the view looked out to surrounding woodland on one side and a crooked little stream running off behind the house and into the fields. Ellen felt herself wavering. Surely, if Warrie had mentioned something about Raoul, she could explain it away so that her beloved would be satisfied. He had met Raoul. There was nothing superficially wrong with seeing an old friend even if she was engaged to be married.

But Ellen could not accept this compromise. Better to lose love and know that she had lost it honestly than to take her share with a deceitful heart. Richard loved her in good faith. She could not besmirch this precious emotion with the filth of her guilty secret.

They were standing in what was going to be Richard's operating room. He was leaning against the wall talking about something that had to do with linoleum, when Ellen interrupted.

"Richard," she said, her voice trembling and hardly above a whisper. "Darling, I want you to listen to me."

He looked at her with surprise. "Am I doing it wrong?" he asked. "Isn't it better to have inlaid than a carpet?"

"This has nothing to do with inlaid," she said. "Richard, I can't marry you."

He stared at her as though she were not speaking English.

"I'm sorry but this can't go on. You've got to know. And I want you to hear it from my own lips. Better for me to tell you face to face than for you to hear it someday from another source."

"What are you talking about, Ellen? Of course you can marry me. You love me, don't you?" He came to her and tried to put his arms around her waist.

"No please," she choked. "Let me go on while I have the courage."

"All right," he said. "Tell me whatever you have to say."

"I've been unfaithful to you," she blurted. Now with the first words spoken, the rest seemed to tumble out by themselves. "All this time I've been going to bed with Raoul Verne. I was going to bed with him a long time before we met and fell in love. Only afterward, I couldn't stop myself. Heaven knows I didn't want to deceive you. But I didn't have the strength. I didn't have the character. You don't know how I hate myself. I wish I had been killed a long time before Raoul came into my life. But it really didn't matter until I met you. And then it was too late."

Ellen stood looking at the bare floor and let the tears run unnoticed down her face. She wasn't crying audibly. The dam of her tortured conscience had simply burst and was spilling its misery unashamed and relentlessly, wringing her of the last drops of guilt.

"I haven't seen him for two weeks," she said in a low voice. "But I never know, from one day to the next, whether I can keep him away. The doorbell and the telephone. He won't let me be because he knows what I am and I'll never change."

Stricken, Richard stood beside her, his hands limp at his sides. She heard him breathing roughly, unable to speak. "I'm not the kind of person you should marry. Please try to forgive me someday and know that I love you with all my heart."

She waited for him to give vent to the white fury that dilated his eyes and made his nostrils flare. If he would slap her, she would feel glad. Instead, he bundled her back into the automobile and took her home.

Ellen sat alone in the growing darkness of oncoming night. She felt strangely at peace with herself. There was nothing to hide anymore. Her secret had been taken from her. Raoul could do nothing anymore to harm her. The husk of her body felt as though it would crumble inward on itself.

She stared vacantly out at the deserted street and watched the inevitable approach of the Cadillac. He could ring the bell into eternity and she would not desire to budge one inch to answer him. Ellen saw Raoul get out of the car and come up the path. Then she heard another car turn into the block. Nita's automobile.

With horrified surprise she saw Dick leap out. He ran and caught up to Raoul just before he reached the door. She saw Dick's fist shoot upward and Ellen whirled away from the window, unable to watch the scene of violence. When she turned back again, both automobiles had driven away.

Ellen went to bed with an almost deathlike peace. The end had come for her. She could sleep now. Raoul would never torment her again. And Dick, perhaps he had achieved a satisfaction. She fell into a heavy and dreamless sleep, glad for the aching loneliness which was her just reward.

The week passed in a gray haze, without event, without thought, without care.

Saturday afternoon the doorbell rang and when she opened it to Richard, Ellen could face him now without flinching.

"I'd like you to come with me," he said.

Ellen agreed. Whatever he wanted from her, she would give completely. If he wished her to pay again and again for her deceit, she would be glad to do this for him.

She got into the car and waited meekly as he drove. She did not often come this way, through the poorest section of town. Rows of wooden houses, blackened from years without paint, sank at strange angles into the ground. They touched and leaned upon each other for help and found none.

"You see," Richard said, "these are the people I'll be treating mostly. They expect me to come in and work miracles for them. In one night I'm supposed to clear away the ravages of malnutrition and uncleanliness."

"That's impossible," she said. "No one can expect that from the greatest doctor."

"We know that. But they do? People always live with the hope that somebody can come and save them."

"Yes, I know what you mean," Ellen said tiredly. "And I for one know that it doesn't work that way."

"Ellen," he pulled the car to the curb. "I can't do everything by myself. All week I've stayed up nights thinking about what it means to love and to trust. I can't work miracles. It won't happen tomorrow. But if we give it time, darling, don't you think we can find our way again?"

Ellen looked at Richard with eyes that would never see beyond him to another man. He leaned across and took Ellen in his arms. Their lips met and they held each other close, oblivious of the hoots of urchins skipping delightedly beside them on the walk.

THE END